PLUCKED

PLUCKED
A Novel in Verse
Vera West

Fictional Café Press

Fictional Café Press
An imprint of Joshua Tree Press, LLP
5 Hollow Lane
Lexington, Massachusetts 024320-3808
jack@fictionalcafe.com

Written, Edited and Printed in the United States of America

ISBN
Print: 979-8-9874421-3-5
eBook: 979-8-9874421-4-2

LCCN: [TK]

For those brave enough to dream again
after waking from a nightmare

PLUCKED

Part One

Calloused fingertips
pluck away
harmonies that
sink into your skin;
whether right or wrong,
each note hurts
more than the last.

1

She has pluck, they say,
with optimism in spades,
surely all her dreams
will come true.

"Iza Jones, are you *scared*?" Tiara quipped.
I'm always nervous
until I step out on to the stage,
until I place the bow to violin,
then the calm washes over me,
a balm on my tight nerves.

"Why couldn't Renée drive you?"
"Wouldn't," I correct.
Renée was my mother;
who'd forbidden my audition.

Tiara laughed,
a trinket of a sound giving away
how insincere she was.
Tiara was that one friend:

> who grew up on your street,
> who played with you out of convenience,
> who you knew was an asshole

but they were your asshole
loyal till the end,
dependable as fuck,
and despite it all,
you'd grown to love them,
that was Tiara.

We had things in common too,
smutty books,
being half-white
without *actually* being white,
jamocha shakes,
celebrity crushes,
and big dreams;
that's where our similarities frayed
and opposites began.

Tiara was prep where I was inner city,
I was kind when Tiara was sharp-tongued,
Tiara was bored when I felt intrigued,
and her white family rejoiced
when mine had denounced.

I didn't feel
any kind of way
about it; these things

were what they were,
and despite it all,
there's always hope:
this audition was tangible *hope*;
a reminder of who I am
—an indisputable fact—
and I'm claiming
what's been ordained *mine*.

No one could stop me,
not even my mother.
I wouldn't allow it.

2

I grew up in the inner city,
a Midwest diamond in the rough
that reverted back to coal
once the automotive industry
pulled out to pull in somewhere else;
factory rats left scurrying
to jobs that soon wouldn't exist;
my mom was one of those rats,
always tittering on about
how she *should have* relocated
(to Hawaii) when they'd offered.

Lucky for us, Mom bought
our beautiful craftsman
before our financial instability
took root, securing the perfect mask
for how poor we were
and how bad things would get;
no one looks too closely at pretty things.
They're accepted as is.

On the same block
at the opposite end
from my house lived Tiara.

Her father was one of those
inferior superior jerks
who was less educated
than he believed and only
became bearable when
his (or his company)
was buzzed; my mother
—cut from a similar cloth—
thought he was great and
Tiara's mother must have
too, because she flitted around
him like a moth to a flame
enamored, but slowly burning up.

Tiara's mom was kind,
with an empathetic generous spirit;
she cooked for me when I visited,
patting my cheek while calling me pretty,
always gushing about
      what a good influence I was,
      what a good friend I was,
and I ate it all alongside the delicious
pancit she'd cook, beaming like a little sun
because I never received praise like that.
It's a powerful thing to be *good enough*.

So while our moms bonded over
spilled tea and hot coffee,
sipping as they endearingly jabbered,
Tiara and I bonded; it was just that simple.

3

My father was a free
spirit turned jaded by
circumstances sprung from
        trauma.
What I mean is,
systematic racism and oppression
shaped his parents, and his parent's parents,
backwards on and on,
unto the very beginning
when our ancestors first
stepped foot on this soil.

It's not an excuse, it's a reason;
sometimes parents are the way they are
'cause *their* parents were the way *they were*.
That's the generational curse: being unable
to become something new,
perpetually stuck being
what our parents, intentionally or
not, made us become.
We're like them, because we are them.

The good news is,

      being *alike* doesn't mean *identical,*
      and sheer will can break the curse.

My grandmother did the best
she could for my father;
I hate clichés, but this time it's true.
Granny was barely my age
when she fell in love,
got married,
fell out of love,
became a barber,
flew north from
Texas to Michigan
and worked — eventually
opening up the Ninth Cat.
You see, she was the ninth
child born and the
barbershop her last life;
it's not an excuse, it's a reason.

I think of the child
version of my father often.
It makes my heart
so full of sadness.
      If only the curse had been broken sooner,
      what a man he could have grown into.

I'm young of course,
not quite eighteen,
and people will say I don't
understand the intricacies,
of *adult* problems, still, I know
doing the right thing is ageless,
being strong isn't tied to brawn,
and wisdom is afforded to all
who seek it.

My fate will be different,
—I'm sure of it—
music is my ticket out,
my magic to finally break the curse.

4

There was nothing cruel or unusual
which justified Renée Boulder
to be cruel or unusual,
she just was.

If you asked my mother directly,
she'd tell you, "I never asked to be
a single mother. That was never the plan."
She pretty much used having a child
as the catalyst for why she'd stopped trying.
I never accepted that truth;
I was just an easy excuse.

Innately, my mother was
one of those people who
wanted everything her way,
and if it couldn't be her way,
clearly, it was *the wrong* way.

My father and Renée met at a nightclub;
something syncopating between
the sips of rum and coke
and the beats of '80s glam rock
seduced them.

"What a time to be alive," Renée said
as I highlighted another line in my textbook.
She always told me about her life
when I was doing something else.
I never knew if it was because
she wanted my attention
or hoped I wasn't really listening.

Their romance had burned
too hot, the kind of unsustainable
flames that will cool to embers;
attraction is never enough,
and the pressure of an unexpected
me led them to realize they'd
never be happy together or apart;
but to amicably separate was doable.

I never saw my father;
he didn't have to stay away
but he chose to.
Everyone said my creativity
—especially music—came from him,
but I wouldn't know.

Like most young mothers
forced to forfeit their dreams

to raise babies, Renée was resentful
and tried to get back what she'd lost
or what she thought she would have
lost if things had worked out,
but if you eat a sandwich,
and you throw it back up
it will never be like it was before.

Renée didn't understand this; trapped
by the past, she never thought
to dream up new dreams.

5

There's a delicate
ecosystem in my household.
Renée bounces from job to job
whereas I clock in as many
hours as I can at Elias Brothers,
our local greasy spoon
turned family restaurant.
I don't mind working;
but my employment feeds
my mother's ambition
to continuously be unemployed.

Appearances are everything,
and Renée, when she is between jobs,
always plays victim of hard times
but the truth is:
      she's never on time,
      moves too slow and,
      has a general disdain
      for authority figures.

The pattern twists on and on,
charms someone into hiring her,
sob stories them into letting her stay,

eventually they get tired of her shit
and fire her anyway.

Meanwhile, she charges me
by the mile for round trip rides
to my greasy-spoon job,
keeping track week by week,
on utility bill return envelopes.

If nothing else, she's a tyrant who's
honorable and fair with record keeping.

Renée tapped the current ledger
a consumer's energy envelope
on the steering wheel;
our old Buick Regal humming as it idled.

"You're already at $17.32," she said,
"it'd be better to pay out with tonight's tips
than wait for the amount to rise."

"I'll pay after my shift," I promised,
"I'll get us Taco Bell on the way home."
Renée's mood perked up;
everyone likes free food.

Renée started to drive,
humming along because
she never remembered lyrics
but dearly loved to sing.
Michael Bolton didn't distract
her as well as he should have.

"You know you're not going
to that school, right?"

She was talking about Everleigh.
I'd hoped if I'd drop it, she'd drop it,
but she wanted assurances
and silence would only provoke her;
lying was hazardous for my nerves,
so I chose a half truth genuine
enough to sound authentic.

"I know you don't want me to go,
and I understand why."

      Renée bit the bait.

"I know music is your dream,"
she admitted, "but dreams
aren't a luxury everyone has.

It's just the two of us,
and we can only make it if we try."

Misquoting Bill Withers
for her own self-serving purposes.

"I know, Mom," I said.
"I'll try to work doubles
 on the weekends."

"You won't need to do doubles
for the whole summer. My last
paycheck will hit the bank soon."

A wise Iza would have stopped talking
but couldn't resist poking the bear.
"Found any good leads for new jobs?"

Renée squinted suspiciously.
"Are you getting jazzy with me?"

Of course I was, but,
of course I said I wasn't.

6

Dishes clanked behind me;
a cook and a busboy
(trying to be a cook)
debating who'd messed up,
while I placed garnishes on
a dinner salad:
two tomatoes,
three cucumbers,
four to eight croutons.
The only rules I followed were these:
people want to eat pretty things,
pretty things make people happy,
happy customers come back.

Everyone hated the night shifts,
but day shifts weren't any better,
the food industry is just grueling
and a bit like the mob,
you can try to leave but
what else is there, especially
for a seventeen-year-old,
on the cusp (hopefully) of college,
I wasn't a long-term investment.

The good news was the owner liked me,
gave me all the hours I wanted,
which had increased dramatically
when my junior year ended
and my last summer started.
The countdown to my escape:
> **three** stay focused,
> **two** save money,
> **one** stick to the plan.

The diner door chimed
—ever notice how all the old doors do?—
and I saw Tiara's familiar face
scanning the room for me.
She spotted me quickly,
telling the hostess to seat her
in my section with a flippant
wave in my direction.

I gathered up my salads
on a tray, added a diet coke
with a lemon wedge
jammed on the cup's edge
and made my way to Tiara
her laptop was already open,
a doc marked in red squiggles

bright on her screen.
Here for the Wi-Fi,
she never came to eat.

"Why do you have to work here again?"
Tiara whined as I set her pop down.
"We could be hanging out *right now*
if you weren't working."

"Evil queen overlord
that only lets me out of my tower
in exchange for coin," I reminded her.

Tiara sighed with forced empathy.
"My father says this isn't the kind of job
for a girl like me."

I controlled my face but my mind yelled:
CRINGE.

"For you," she quickly explained,
"it's different of course. Too bad you can't
run away."

I tapped my apron pocket where
my acceptance letter was peeking out.

"My escape is pending."

If it sounds arrogant, then it probably is,
but I'd known I'd impressed the judges.

There'd been an energy in the air
as my right arm, ebbed and flowed
the bow over the strings;
as my left hand's fingers
found the intonation
time and time again,
I knew my time had come.
This was *it*,
and when the letter came,
I opened it knowing
already what it'd say.

Tiara leaned forward excitedly
nearly tipping her coke.
"You got accepted?" she whispered.

I nodded and Tiara shook her head.
"She'll never let you go."

Movement in my peripheral
alerted me to my boss heading

my way, so I winked at Tiara,
—code for, *I've got this*—
and made my way back
to the kitchen just as the
cook yelled order up.

I did have a plan,
but it relied heavily
on the help of two
unpredictable forces,
Tiara and my father.

7

Days turned to weeks,
weeks to months,
and too quickly I was down
to just a handful of days before
the new school year started.

I slowed down,
dwindling my hours
so I wouldn't put anyone
in a big bind when I left;
I had just shy of a fortnight
(fancy regency talk for two weeks)
before I had to get to Everleigh.

I'd been stalling
but I couldn't avoid pleading
with Tiara to drive me;
so on an unexpected Saturday night
I "wasn't" able to secure a
double shift, I shot my shot.

"I'm like your personal chauffeur now?"
Tiara scoffed. She wasn't mad,
she'd never admit it but she thrived on

being needed, and I was pretty sure
she'd say yes—after hazing me of course.

"You're the only one I can trust," I reminded her.
"True," Tiara agreed, "but what do I tell your
mom
when she wants to know where you are?"
"Tell her the truth. It won't matter by then."

Tiara licked her lips between nibbles
of salt and vinegar chips,
pretending to draw out her answer.
I already knew she would;
she only put on theatrics for yeses.
Even so, a sweetened deal never hurt.

"I'll pay you for gas
and your time," I bargained.
Tiara scoffed.
"I'll drive you but I
don't *need* your money."

I whooped in triumph!

"What do you want then?"
"…your soul," Tiara said in a creepy voice,

more hoarse than scary,
"but I'll settle for first dibs on any
cute artsy boys you meet."

I laughed. "You've got to be
the weirdest person I've ever
known."
"That's because you know
like two people, but fine,
I'll settle for you owing me one."

"Just add it to my tab!" I teased.
"One day I'll cut you off,
and I won't give it a second
thought," Tiara replied.
"Do you give any decision
of yours a second thought?"
Tiara shook her head.
"My natural decisiveness is
one of my greatest attributes."
"You just don't want
your free diet coke train
to end."
Tiara nodded with a sigh.
"You're not wrong.

I haven't had to pay for a diet
coke in years."

Our chatter died down
as reruns of *Degrassi* started
to play. I stayed another hour
or so, wanting to go home
but not wanting to come off
as a leech either; I wasn't
the mooch-and-run type.

8

I hated the city bus;
the sticky floors,
the lurking men
staring from faded plastic
seats. It creeped me out,
but it couldn't be avoided.
With my ride secured,
the next complication
to iron out was a
parental signature on
Everleigh's admission forms.
I couldn't transfer without it.

The bus stopped
at the Ninth Cat,
my granny's barbershop
on the corner of a
rundown street
in my rundown town,
but its faded red paint
shone like a ruby to me;
its twisting red, blue, white
barber sign, a beacon
in the community.

The shop was her pride
and I was her joy.

—ding, ding, ding—
chimed the old door's bell.
Granny was with a customer,
but she set down her clippers
to give me a side hug
—always careful to never
get hair on her grandbabies—

An oscillating fan blew,
swaying my prized
kindergarten finger painting
back and forth on its
Scotch-tape hooks.
She'd hung it up almost
thirteen years ago;
they just don't make
tape like that anymore.

"Shouldn't you be at school, baby?"
I shook my head, "Class ended
 at three."

Granny started the clippers again,
the hum not too loud
for me to talk
or for her to hear.

"I got accepted into a music school,"
I blurted out; sometimes,
the best way to say something
was to just say it.

Granny's ears perked,
her eyes shimmered.
"College?"
I shook my head.
"It's a school that preps you for college."
She frowned, her glimmer
dimming to worry,
and told me it sounded *expensive*.
I explained the scholarships,
the opportunity to work,
and she beamed again.
Hardworking women
respect opportunities
and my granny, Mert Jones,
was the hardest working
of us all.

Granny paused cuttin' hair
and watched me.
"Your momma won't let you go,
and you need your daddy to sign?"
I nodded.
"Can you leave the form?"
I shook my head.

Granny leaned forward to her customer,
told him she'd be back in five;
loyal customers never minded.

She took off her apron
with an idle sweep,
shaking the soft black
puffs of hair onto the floor
and motioned for me to follow her.

In the back of the store,
was the *other store*,
Granny's second job: selling Avon
and she was damn good.
When I was little, she watched me
on afternoons and weekends;
I'd count inventory for her,
tallying up roll-on deodorants and perfumes

as we ate fries and hamburgers,
chugging pop and crunching ice,
plucking lottery numbers
out of the sky (sure to win)
and jotting them down in a worn notebook.
Today she got a pen and held her hand out.

"Give me that form," Granny said smirking,
"and this stays between us, you hear?"
She signed my father's name
in a pretty penmanship that made
me wonder if cuttin' hair had really
been her dream.

I thanked her and
then thanked her again as she
filled a grocery bag with toiletries, and
handed me a bundle of rolled twenties,
eyes gleaming with pride.

I didn't often ask but when I did,
Granny always came through.

9

The week leading up
to my escape to Everleigh
flew.

I'd been stuffing items into
my purse piece by piece,
stashing them in a
duffle bag I'd hidden
deep in the storage room
at Elias Brothers.

I was Tom Cruise in
the role of Ethan Hunt,
sneaking around,
being clever as fuck;
It was a good look for me,
at least in my opinion.

Taking care of my gas tithe early,
I'd successfully buttered
up my mom, and the additional
money I was able to give her
got her to jubilantly agree
to what she believed was a
weekend hoorah with Tiara.

As far as Renée knew,
she'd drop me off at work Friday,
Tiara would pick me up after my shift
and I'd be home Sunday afternoon.

It was the perfect setup,
with cash and over thirty-six
hours to pretend she wasn't a mom,
Renée would suspect nothing and
I could freely capitalize on her oblivion
to achieve my American dream.
Skewed, yet oddly poetic in its irony.

I'd been up to other stuff as well,
like opening a bank account,
changing from check to direct deposit,
researching getting a driver's license,
but that would be something to tackle later
and I was fine with that; emancipation was a
process.

I'd lied about having to work tonight too;
the manager on duty scrunched his
face when he saw me walk in.
"Forgot my bag," I explained
and scurried away from

the echo of, "Aren't you on summer break?"
I grabbed my duffle bag,
hauling it over my shoulder with a *huff*.
It had filled up quick.

I went out the back exit,
ignoring the busboy leaning against
the faded building wall as he called
out that he thought I wasn't working tonight.
I guess Renée was the only one
not paying attention.

I spotted Tiara's Subaru parked
at a pump waiting for me at
the gas station next door
and picked up my pace.

Brain told me it was unlikely
I'd get caught; there was no one
to ask me where I was going
or what I was doing, but my heart
felt calmer with every foot farther
away from Elias Brothers;
eager to hit the road.

Tiara waved as I approached,
the pump clicking methodically
as it filled the tank.

"Stay here while I get snacks," Tiara said,
skipping off before I could respond.

I watched the numbers rise
a reverse countdown until
I could get in the car.

A male voice crooned behind me.
"Do you come here often?"
Renée giggled.
"To the *gas station*? About once a week in fact."
A slew of *fuckity fuck fucks* blared
through my head while they chatted,
I wasn't sure what was more horrifying;
the way my mom flirted
or the fact that she was here
pumping gas right behind me.

I forced an outward calm
I clearly didn't feel, walked
around to the passenger side
and got in.

Tiara came back,
tossing bags of
spicy nacho Doritos
and sour Skittles
through the open window
onto my lap.

She scowled at me.
"You forgot to hook the pump up."
"Just get in the car," I snapped,
my uncharacteristic tone
spurring her into action, she holstered
the pump and got behind the wheel.

I jutted a thumb behind me.
"It's my mom," I said.
"Who's that guy? He's *not* cute."
"Can we just go?" I pleaded.
Tiara nodded and we pulled off,
but I swear, as the car moved
my mom looked over
and our eyes locked, couldn't say
if it was a second or thirty
but I know she saw me
at the same moment her *man*
tucked a loose strand of hair

behind her ear, and she turned
back towards him with a blush,
too smitten to care that I'd lied to her.

It stung—the awareness of her
rejection or perhaps it was her lack of care—
but it also freed me;
putting myself first was a
choice I was making too.

10

There were plot twists in my story,
truths most people would never realize;
one of them how my parents' romance
had caused a Shakespearean-sized riff.

Renée came from a
large, traditional white family
and while an interracial boyfriend
was a cute rebellion,
an interracial baby went *too far*;
Her family demanded a fix for her blunder.

When my mother refused to
terminate the pregnancy or
give me up for adoption,
her family gave her tough love:
       they disowned her.

I didn't mean it figuratively
when I said it was just the two of us.

The only things I knew about Renée's family
were reminiscent tidbits,
yet despite knowing I couldn't,

I dreamed up of ways
I could change their minds,
show them how valuable
a little black girl could be.

I know it doesn't work that way
but outcasted things long to belong.

Then, when I was eight
I found my way, *music,*
one sunny afternoon
during a gymnasium
instrumental demonstration,
they introduced the children
of William Frantz Elementary
to a clarinet, and a trumpet,
and a flute, and a trombone,
and a violin.

I saw the violin and it was the same
violin from the bedtime tidbit
my mom had told me about
her father who'd played violin,
who'd been a virtuoso in his time,
and felt relieved, joy even,
because I'd found my way in;

they'd accept me through music.

My mother loved the idea
and happily paid the
fifteen-dollars-a -year
instrument rental fee.
Being a classical violinist
was a testament to my intellect,
a safe harbor from my
genetically preconditioned
curses (you know, black folks are
aggressive, animalistic,
unmotivated, uneducated,
the boys fast at athletics,
but the girls just *fast* in general).

If I could conquer this instrument
it would redeem us both.
Renée would keep me safe.

11

My nerves exponentially settled
with every streetlight
between us and the gas station.
"Don't you need to stop somewhere?" Tiara asked.
I nodded. "The pawnshop on Fifth.
I need to pick up my violin."

"Don't you have a violin?"
Tiara asked in confusion.
"You know, that four-stringed instrument
you auditioned with at the beginning
of summer?"

"I *had* a violin, smart-ass,
but it was a school rental."

Putting the car in park,
Tiara smirked, "I didn't think you were
that poor? How is it even possible
with how much you work?"

I didn't answer her,
I was an avid believer
that when someone was

deliberately being an ass,
it was your duty to ignore them.

Tiara hadn't really expected
an answer, she just trotted behind me
into the pawnshop, mumbling
complaints about how
thick and dusty the air was.

She was right about that;
the air felt dry and thick
and just…not fresh.
I held in a cough and
approached the clerk.
I tapped my fingers
rhythmically
against the plexiglass counter.
I couldn't believe I'd pulled any of this off.
Music = freedom.

"How can I help you, miss?"
I grinned. "I need to pay off a violin."
He nodded, took my name,
and began the process.

"Make sure it's all there,"

he advised without looking up,
"no refunds on instruments."

It was: pegs, strings, bridge, sound post.
I studied the bow: horse hair, robust and clean.
I plucked each string: Aa, Dd, Gg, Ee.
The shop was quiet,
everyone watching and waiting.
"Play it if you want," the clerk said.
I put bow to string,
vibrations erupting into the air
a swirl of woman-made tones.
I made it sound good
and I knew this
violin and I would
work.

12

Tiara had offered to walk around,
to take in the sights and smells,
but I'd wanted to experience
Everleigh, the dawning
of my new life alone.

She was pissed,
probably feeling used
or ditched or unneeded,
but I was oblivious,
already in awe of the
world around me.

Tucked away
in green
trees and grass,
this place was more
oasis than school;
students bustling around
like uniform ants
(a uniform, shit, I'd have to
sort that out)
arms full of books,
(textbooks, double shit)

smiling and waving
as their paths to
class overlapped,

> Thumping heart
> and beaded sweat,
> anxiety held my breath.

I adjusted my duffle bag,
repositioning both it and
my violin case strap
to another equally
tender spot on my shoulder.
I was royally screwed,
wondering how
I'd had the audacity
to think this was possible.

—THUMP—
a pressure hit my back,
and like in some '90s
rom-com, I was thrust forward
only to be anchored back
against the clumsy boy
who'd knocked me over
in the first place.

Yes, I knew it was a boy,
call me now: Miss Cleo.

"Are you okay?"
I asked even though *he*
should have asked.

"I'm Apollo and yes,
you're fine, I'm fine—I'm okay.
Is your violin okay?"

Brown skin,
broad shoulders,
black curls,
blushed cheeks.
Apollo *was fine*
and forgiven.

I hadn't dropped my case
but Apollo and I had smashed
into it like a sandwich;
couldn't hurt to check.
I placed it on the ground
and opened the case.

I peeked inside:
the sound post was still posted,
the neck wasn't severed,
no snapped strings,
no popped pegs,
no broken bridge.

"It looks okay," Apollo assessed,
peering over my shoulder.
"All's well that ends well," I agreed.
"A violin by any other name would
still sound as sweet," Apollo said.
I turned to stare at him,
such a corny twist of Bill Shakes
deserved attention and he
looked very pleased with himself.
"You started it," he said, "by the way,
you never told me your name."

"Knocking into a fellow musician?"
a cheery voice called. "Hi, I'm Artemis,
is my evil twin causing a catastrophe?"

I blinked.
Apollo nodded empathetically.
"Our parents were mythology enthusiasts."

"One might say *geek* enthusiast,"
quipped a new female voice.
The twins groaned in unison.
"Don't scowl, Artie, introduce me!
It looks like she's another violinist."

Her name was Belinda Gris
(like the Spanish word for *grey*,
but their last name had creole roots;
romantic languages and all that)
she was their mother,
and she did an excellent
monologue of their origin story:

>Artemis Gris, preferred name: Artie,
>fellow violinist,
>Apollo Gris, preferred name: Apollo,
>creative writer,
>were just joining Everleigh, like I was,
>for their senior year.

>Apparently, affirmative action had
>made the way for minority
>students to attend in their senior
>year: Everleigh checked out a box,
>and we check into self-doubt,

> forever wondering if we'd earned this
> spot or been given it;
> that's how the game's played.

It was determined that we were
all headed in the wrong direction
to the same place and decided
to sojourn together.

"With our luck," Artie beamed,
"we'll be roommates."
I nodded, hopeful for that outcome,
quick to latch on to anything familiar.
"You still haven't told us your name,"
Apollo reminded me teasingly.
I'm Iza Jones and I'm going to make it.

Part Two

Each plucked feather
stings and the stings
don't fade like you
assume they would;
they burn, ripening
into a pain that
makes you numb, and
becomes your new normal.

13

She was plucked, they whispered,
spilling tea; they brewed
concocted tales
of how she came to be.

Orientation was brief,
held in a giant gym-like room,
consisting of haughty airs,
and dull droning speeches
from past educators and
celebrity alumni; all
creating an ambiance of
imposter syndrome
reminding me how out
of my league I was.
A woman at a check-in table
passed out thick packets,
and name tags.

Artie saved me a seat,
commandeering my packet
and only mere seconds later
whooping loudly as she
waved my housing sheet,

like a victory flag.
Belinda shushed her quietly
as she confirmed our golden luck,
"We're roommates, Iza!" Artie
cheered in whispered tones.

I spun the dorm key on my finger,
watching it loop 'round and 'round
the orbit I'd created.

Apollo was quiet beside me,
as we listened to Artie chirp away.
Belinda eyeballed me,
watching or rather studying me,
sizing me up,
weaving assumptions
about my past-present-future.

"Your parents
couldn't make it?" Belinda asked.
I shook my head.

She motioned towards
the duffle bag at my feet,
"All your stuff is in there?" she asked.
I nodded yes.

An eternity passed,
staring each other down.
Belinda must be suspicious now.
I was tense, bracing for
(judgmental) impact when
 she finally made her move.

"Would you like to get dinner with us?"

I hadn't expected *that*;
kindness is always
a surprise, isn't it?
I surprised myself too
by saying *yes.*
It's not like I knew them,
but I was hungry and
a free meal was
one less meal I had to pay for.

I spent the rest of orientation
thinking about the *why*
behind Belinda.
I had a few guesses:
        she wanted to help a fellow minority,
        she was an *actual* Christian,
        she felt sorry for me,

she needed a pet project,
they could all be wrong or true,
and it mattered.
I needed to know her reason
so I would know how to respond.

But a tiny voice whispered
she could just be a nice human
without an agenda,
who cared for other humans.

I'd always wondered
what *those kind of parents* were like,
the kind whose knee-jerk reaction
was to help, rather than hurt or hinder.

My mind kept spiraling,
spinning during the campus tour,
thinking about all the *ifs*
that could occur at dinner, until
I had a few scenarios plotted out:
if they asked about my past,
if they asked about my present,
if they asked about my future,
then I'd politely deflect to other topics;
that's what I *should* do,

it'd be the best way to
safeguard my first impression.

"Earth to Iza!" Artie sang teasingly.
I mumbled an apology,
pasted a smile,
pushed down my feelings,
then I realized Artie had been
asking if I'd rather drop our
stuff off now or after dinner.
The thought of food
made my stomach gurgle.

Belinda blasted me with a smile.
She missed nothing and like all
good moms, had a witty one-liner
on standby, "Well, I guess
that answers it," she said, motioning
to my stomach that of course,
on cue, groaned again.

14

We pulled up into an
Elias Brothers and I snorted.
Apollo peeked over his shoulder
from the front seat and I
clamped a hand over my mouth.
As Belinda shifted the car into park,
Artie whispered from beside me,
"Are you okay?"

Tell her, don't tell her…
tell her, don't tell her…
don't–
just tell her!

"I used to work at one of these
back home," I blurted out.
"Wanna eat somewhere
else then?" Artie asked.
I shook my head no,
she shrugged,
and we went in.

This one must've been corporate owned,
the seats still plump,

window ledges not faded,
computers actually responsive.

They had an atrium,
no ponds or greenery
but ceiling-to-floor windows.
My mom would have called it a patio,
but that wasn't quite right either.

The hostess seated us there
of course, making small
talk as she wove her way,
through the tables and booths.
It was odd to be on the other side.

"What's good here, Iza?"
Artie asked, scanning the menu.
Belinda asked if I'd been here before,
which prompted Artie to explain
and Apollo to ask if I
wanted to eat somewhere else,
but I promised it was fine
since we were already seated.

We all ordered:
        patty melt for Belinda,

       spaghetti no meatballs for Artie,
       Slim Jim sandwiches for Apollo and I.
Apollo had good taste in food,
I'd never tell him
the sandwiches were stored
(hoagie bun, meat, cheese and all)
in a refrigerated drawer.

They all added the salad bar too;
endless fruits, cold salads,
cream of broccoli soup,
a $5.99 up-charge I never added
even with my discount.
After smelling, serving food
all day, it was hard to eat.
Apollo and Artie sprinted away
to fill their plates,
leaving Belinda and I alone to wait.

"Can I be frank?" Belinda asked.
I gave a hesitant nod,
rolling the paper straw wrapper
between my fingers
until it twisted into a thread.

"You don't seem
to be in a good way,"
Belinda said softly,
"and I don't know you well
(yet) but my gut tells me
you could use someone
looking out for you.
You've got a good energy
about you, Iza, and I promise
I'll do what I can for you.
You just focus on learning
all you can at Everleigh, okay?"
She gave my hand a pat
and scooted her chair
back to stand.

"Have the waitress add
the salad bar to your dinner;
it's a steal at $5.99."

15

City mouse made it
to *the Mark,*
the most successful
retail department store
chain in America
branded by a red bullseye.

My mother had always
preferred the department stores
with "mart" at the end of their name,
or rather that's where she
could afford to go.

It felt silly to have wanted to
come to a store like this.
This was a *normal store*
but it hadn't been accessible
to me, not with all the weight
placed on my shoulders
by shitty parents
who couldn't be bothered.

As I followed like an
ugly duckling behind

Belinda, Artie and Apollo,
the industrial store lights
felt too bright,
the chilled AC air
felt too cool,
and then not cool at all.
I felt *hot*; when did it get warm?
My brown hands
had begun to shake,
quivering with an
overwhelming sense of panic
I didn't know how to turn off.

Could I even turn it off?
I took a breath,
then another,
and another,
one more, deep and slow,
yet the world still spun.

This had to be a panic attack.
I was young for a stroke,
        right?
Right, I thought,
answering myself.

"You'll need some bedding,
toiletries, snacks, maybe some
cute little twinkle lights," Belinda
assessed.
"We're not twelve," Apollo mumbled.
"I'll take his twinkle lights," Artie said.
And just like that,
I felt normal again,
successfully shoving down
whatever emotion
had tried to bubble up.
I ran my fingertips
over the many comforters
until I touched the right one.

16

I was wrong,
I wasn't done panicking yet.
I felt another wave, triggered
by the sheer amount of
"for Iza" items Belinda
had tossed into the cart.

She knew, and she *knew*
I knew she knew too.
It was evident in the
pats on my arm,
the worried mom looks,
the encouraging me to
pick something out
of *this and that* until
I literally had all the
this and that
that the store carried.
No shelf was left untouched
and I'd never be able to pay
her kindness back.

By the time we'd made it
to the checkout line
I had a headache.

By the time the
items were sliding
down the conveyor belt
I felt lightheaded.

By the time the
rhythmic beeping of items
being rung up were bagged
I was nauseous.

Apollo swept past me,
grabbing my hand
on the way, while
simultaneously swiping
a water bottle.

"Iza and I are going
to wait outside," he called
over our shoulders.

I couldn't do anything
other than hiccup,
which was just
a failing attempt to not cry.
I wasn't even a crier.

"What the fuck am I doing?"
I gasped, exasperated.

"Having a panic attack," Apollo
said matter-of-factly. "I've been
watching you no, too creepy,
I've been paying attention
to you and I know
we literally don't know
each other but, Iza, what's going on?"

I shook my head;
talking led to
sharing which led to
crying which led to
embarrassing myself
in front of a stranger
whose sister was my roommate,
in this small world where we
all went to the same bougie school.

I paced instead.
Apollo held out
the water to me
and I took it

but couldn't
even open it,
all I could do
was keep moving.

He caught my wrist
and gave it a little
tug that sent me
off my path
and on to his,
past his arms,
into a hug;
a hug, I thought,
when was the last time
I'd been hugged?

He said nothing.
He was just there,
stranger to stranger.

Who hugged people they
didn't even know?
I realized my arms
were just dangling, like I was
a broken doll who couldn't
hug back, but the longer

we stood there, the more
I really needed that hug
and slowly I wrapped
my arms around him too;
and then
that muthafucker squeezed,
leveling up the hug
and I was obliterated.

"It's okay to cry, Iza," Apollo
said quietly.
"No it isn't," I choked out.
"If you can't tell me, tell Artie, okay?"

I kept crying,
he kept holding,
until eventually I was out of tears
and felt like I could breathe again.

"Let's go sit in the car," Apollo said.
He held my hand, leading me away
from the store entrance and
back to his mother's car.

"Do you even have the car keys?" I asked.
"She never locks the car."
"Must be nice," I muttered,
"where I'm from, that's an invitation
for a stolen vehicle."
Apollo smiled.
"I wouldn't advise stealing
my mom's car, she really likes you."
I laughed, unable to stop.
The joke wasn't funny
but low-key it kind of was.

"I must be losing my mind,"
I whispered, wiping away
remnants of old and new tears.

"Everything's going to be okay."
"You don't even know what's wrong," I said.
"*Tao of Pooh*, ever read it?" Apollo asked.
I shook my head.
"I'll lend you my copy."

17

The whole gang had
to carry bags in order
for our haul to be
brought up in one trip.
Quickly afterwards,
Apollo ushered his mom away
—I was thankful for that—
as the dorm door closed
Belinda tried to whisper,

> *look out for her,*
> *she doesn't have anyone,*

but Artie heard it too,
giving me a sympathetic glance
before busying herself.

It was disarming
how easily they'd guess,
how easily I'd been read;
it made me feel pathetic.
Crying was a loss of control,
loss of control was weakness,
and I hated being weak.

But it was more than that.
A part of me was grieving my
old life, how easily it'd let me go,
like it hadn't wanted me anyway.

18

I was done crying,
my eyes red,
tender from rubbing;
my phone had no
missed calls or messages.
My gut clenched,
I'd made my bed,
now I had to lay in it.

I'd finished making my
real bed (not proverbial)
and it felt foreign.
The bedding doused
in a plastic-bag smell
that would take
many washes to purge.

Artie was sitting
on her adjacent bed
reading a worn
Pride and Prejudice,
probably her favorite.
I had a similar looking *Frankenstein,*
worn and faded in my duffle bag.

I wasn't surprised she didn't
use an e-reader; she had
a hipster page-turner vibe,
whereas I was just broke.

I shattered the silence when
I realized Artie was reading
but never turning a page.

"I really appreciate what
your mom did for me today."

Relief swept across Artie's face.
"You're not mad? I assumed
That was why you were upset?"

I shook my head, *feeling full,*
a term Southern ladies
used to describe emotions
so overwhelming,
so tangled and raw,
that all you can do is
feel what you feel.
       You had to sit in it.

Artie looked like she understood
everything I wasn't saying.
"We all have our trials,
but if we stick together,
help each other,
be encouraging,
in the end we'll be stronger.
I don't need to know
your story to know
that you're strong, Iza,
and my family will
do what we can
to help you."

I laughed, a mix of
bitterness and relief;
"Your family always
rescues strays?"

Artie smirked,
"You're here, Iza,
you already rescued yourself."

19

I slept hard that night,
waking up in the morning
to my buzzing phone
tucked under my pillow.

It was *Granny*;
wondering how I was,
asking if I'd eaten,
telling me momma was furious,
but also reminding me
how proud she was.

"You're doing
what you're designed to do,"
Granny said, "believe that, Iza."

I wanted to believe,
but I was scared,
how many chances did a
brown girl from a poor town get?
ONE.

Artie was brown too,
but it was different for her;

she was brown with money.
Her seat was secure, at least,
as long as she had
the talent to back it up.

A million things could go wrong
for me; being able to keep up
with these kids was only the start.

"Apollo wants to walk around,"
Artie said, "get a feel for Everleigh.
You wanna come with us?"

I nodded.
It wasn't a bad idea,
getting the lay of the land,
avoiding the sound of my thoughts;
if I was with Artie and Apollo, I could
focus on them and not myself.

20

Everleigh's campus was more
junior college than high school
with its separate buildings for:
      general classes,
      a kaiju-sized library,
      a performance hall
      and arts center;
what an amazing
resource, a hidden oasis
for developing talent,
and I got to go here.

I was a mix of awe
and apprehension.
It's easy to build yourself
up to chase the dream,
but once you've caught it
that was another level.

Artie had printed our
schedules and our
first mission was winning
the scavenger hunt
of locating all of our classes.

"What kind of writer
are you, Apollo?" I asked
as we walked.

Smirking, a brilliant blaze, he shrugged,
"The writing kind."

I must have gawked,
because I don't have a poker face,
and because Artie laughed, saying,
"Same look Mom gives him
when he's being faux philosophical.
I prefer his prose to his poetry,
Mom prefers his boring essays and
Apollo just prefers to write."

Apollo checked his watch.
"We have just enough time
to check out textbooks
before the library closes."
"And then, we can ditch you
and check out the dungeons," Artie added.
the dungeons:
       a beloved slang term
       (by both student and faculty)
       that described the various

> study areas, art studios, music rooms
> located beneath the dorms.

Admittedly, I did want to see them.
I was itching to play;
eager to calm my nerves
soothe my mind,
let the familiarity
ground me.

21

We left Apollo behind,
eyes glazed as he skimmed
through the index of
a fifty-dollar copy of
African American Poetry:
250 Years of Struggle and Song.
His enthusiasm was more
convincing than any blurb
could've been, but there
was nothing strong
enough to tempt me into
tackling a five-hundred
page book by choice;
I had commitment issues.

"My precious," sneered Artie,
(in a spot-on Sméagol voice),
tugging on my sleeve, she added,
"Come on! It'll be eons before he
resurfaces from that book."
"I'm like that with violin,
everything fades when I play."

We dropped our books off,
swapping our backpacks
for music cases and
headed to the dungeons.

My imagination was disappointed.
I'd been ready for creepy crawly
but the dungeons gave zero
haunted-house bad-basement vibes.
Nope, they were windowless,
each room generously spacious
affording every student a
desk, chair, stand and
weighted-keys electric piano;
Casio, eat your heart out.

I began unpacking my
violin, idly plucking
each string, testing
how out of tune it was: woof.
Artie leaned against the wall,
holding her case in front
as she nodded towards
my instrument.

"What kind of violin is that?"
I smirked. "The pawnshop kind."

Artie grinned back, making a chef's kiss
as she pushed away from the wall.
"I've got an extra set of strings
you can have," she sang as she left,
"and if the pegs keep slipping
try rubbing a little chalk
or rosin on them."

An hour later
I was doing exactly that,
and also praying
to any available gods
that my pegs would stop slipping.
Sure, the violin didn't
make the musician
but a good one sure did help.

I decided to take a break,
sitting on the floor cross-legged
and rubbing the tension out of
my left hand's fingers.

Artie was working on a
repetitive-sounding piece
that was probably an étude
or a bow practice; she made
it sound like *music* rather than
a practice of vigor.

My stomach twisted
as my brain whispered,
Are you good enough?

I hopped back up,
feeling a renewed
determination to prove
that *yes,* I was enough.
I returned again
and begun a slow Bach
piece I knew by heart,
testing the limits of myself
and my instrument,
and it began to flow better,
and the more I relaxed
the better I sounded
which of course made me
feel better too.

I shook off my doubts
and let those harmful
raindrops soak the ground
rather than me.
I'd known this
wouldn't be easy
but I was willing to
fight for this dream.

22

The music theory class began
at 7:57 a.m., a full 180 seconds
before class officially started.

Artie rolled her eyes, mumbling,
        and so it begins,
as we scurried to
the closest seats.
We'd both overslept,
missing mess hall breakfast,
but I was the only one who
took it as an omen for the day.

"What are the three
principles of music theory?"
our teacher asked.
        Sight Singing
        Keyboard
        and Theory,
he answered before
any of us took
a breath to speak.

"I'm Professor Maclean
and I am not your friend.
I am a resource designed
to help you become
a *true* musician."

If *unimpressed* was a person
he was standing before us
in a stretched taut,
tucked-in polo shirt with
a look of snobby disdain
plastered on his face.

"Christ in a handbasket,"
mumbled Artie behind me.

"Christ wouldn't fit in a handbasket,"
Maclean roared, "nor would he find
that cheeky comment comical.
You're new to Everleigh,
what's your name?"

It took a heartbeat
and for me to realize
he was talking to me,

which meant he didn't
realize that snark had
come from Artie.

"Iza Jones," I stammered.

"Please join us in front of
the class to demonstrate
your prowess at sight singing."

I heard Artie whisper
a quick *sorry* but it was
too late for me, I knew
this wasn't ending well.
I'd never been able
to carry a tune.

Maclean smirked;
walking over to
an upright piano
tucked in a corner
he hit middle C
and then headed to
the white board (conveniently
embedded with a music staff)

and wrote the symbols to indicate:
bass clef,
common time,
key of c-minor,
and a slew of scribbled
notes in various rhythms.
He even had the audacity
to draw some connecting
lines for phrasing.
      My goose was cooked.

Maclean clicked the cap
back on his marker and
tapped the board indignantly:
"Now, sing *Christ in a handbasket*."

I peered at the board,
the writing swirling
like an elusive
mathematical equation;
music written for a violin
was always in treble clef;
I couldn't easily read
bass, especially under
pressure.

"Professor, it wasn't Iza
who made that comment,
it was me," Artie confessed.

"I see, I'm to be insulted
twice, first with poor manners
and now by the assumption
I don't know what I heard?
Speak out of turn again
and you'll be performing
Lakmé "duo des fleurs"
with your friend."

I took a breath and sang
and whatever came out
was neither planned nor in tune.

The class erupted in laughter,
and a satisfied Maclean
let me take my seat.

23

Private lessons were next,
and I prayed Jesus was out of
his handbasket, ready to help
turn this day around from its
shit-show sight-singing start.

Lana Grande (my instructor)
was young for her field
due to being a child prodigy.

By two she was playing,
by ten she was performing,
by seventeen she was winning
Tchaikovsky competitions in Russia.

I was impressed with her,
although she didn't seem
overly impressed with me;
she was intrigued and had
questions.

"Private lessons?"
"None."
"Suzuki method proficiency?"

"Barely."
"Can you play scales?"
"Like a boss."
Lana frowned, "What does that mean?"
"I'm proficient in scales," I explained.
"Play your audition piece."

Finally! A chance for her to see
how I'd made it to Everleigh
and Lana did seem pleased,
but still not impressed enough
to resist stopping me before
I'd even made it halfway through.

"You have raw talent
but you lack technique.
We must start over,
from the beginning.
It'll be hard,
you'll be frustrated, but if
you commit to my methods,
I will teach you."

I nodded enthusiastically;
I'd do anything for this dream.

"I'm going to give you a list of
books to buy—"
I interjected, asking if
they could be borrowed.
Lana frowned, as if the thought
had never occurred to her
to borrow a book.

"Is money an issue?" she asked.
"Yes," I responded just as bluntly.
"Explains a lot," she murmured
eyeing my violin, "but I admire
your tenacity. You're determined
and that's a significant quality
you'll need to go pro."

She thought for a moment,
her eyes shifting between
me,
my violin,
and somewhere else entirely
before settling concretely back on
me.

"I often get gifted
violins; usually

it's tied to an endorsement
but it's resulted in a surplus
of dusty instruments.
I'll bring a couple
that you can keep
as long as you promise
to take my instruction seriously.
You'll need to practice
two hours daily and triple that
on the weekends.
No boys either, they're just
distractions."

I thanked her a million times over,
my failings this morning
made distant memory.
I'd never had someone
rally behind me like this,
helping me help myself.
I just had to work hard,
and that had always been
my superpower.

As I put away my violin
I felt the vibrations of
my cell buzzing in my pocket.

Tiara was calling but hung up
before I could answer.
How odd, she never called,
she was that friend *you* had to call
who'd whine you hadn't called sooner.
I had a few unread texts too; she must be bored.
I stuffed my phone away and headed to my next
class.

24

—buzz, buzz—,
in my pocket again,
Tiara wouldn't stop calling.
I sent her to voicemail,
and silenced my phone.

25

By urban standards
this was a restaurant
not a cafeteria and
to top it off, everything
was free!

Isn't it funny how
people who don't
need free *get free*?
Well, I suppose I was
getting free when I needed it.

Bougie as it was,
I still felt like
Bella in *Twilight*
trying to navigate
my way through a sea
of established cliques.

Artie rescued me
(of course)
waving me over
to a table filled
with strangers

she'd already
gotten to know.
Apollo wasn't there.
Artie read my mind,
gave a little smirk as she said,
"He usually skips
lunch, goes to the
library instead."

"I have work-study
in the library, so
I'll probably see him."

Artie grinned,
saying nothing,
but looking like:
mmmm hmmm.

I felt myself blush
and changed the
unspoken subject.

"Met your teacher yet?" I asked.
Artie nodded, "Apparently
I got everyone's favorite

swoony *Joshua Bell* vibes
professor."

I crinkled my nose.
"I'm more of a
Damien Escobar fan."
Artie laughed.
"I could've guessed."

"I got assigned to
the child prodigy
violinist."

Artie and everyone else gasped.

"She's everyone's pick,"
said a girl with ashy-red
pigtailed buns.

"But she's also a little
off if you know what I mean,"
another girl chimed in.

"She did seem intense,"
I admitted, "but the only
way out is through, right?"

"Not really," someone else
chimed in, "you can always
request a different teacher."

But I'd never want
another teacher,
I wanted gasp-worthy,
the legend,
the teacher who'd mold me
into a real musician
and I wasn't the
this is hard so I give up
kind of girl.

"One way or another,"
I declared to the
table that had already
switched to a new topic,
"I'll see this through to the end."

26

Apollo was seated at
a large oak table
when I walked into
the library for work-study.

I beelined to him,
placing chips and
a bottled water
I'd commandeered
from the mess hall.
"Have you been here
since lunch?" I whispered.
He smirked, "How? I have classes."
"Special writer shit or something,"
I whispered back, "how would I know?"

"Iza Jones?" the librarian called
from the front desk.
"Yes, hi, sorry, that's me!"
She beckoned me over
and I scurried away,
leaving a smirking
Apollo to his books.

"I'm Mrs. Sullivan."
She pointed to the front
desk, "your advisor
is here to see you,"
and jerked a thumb
back behind her.
"Come find me in the
back when you're
done."

I nodded and strode away.
I was aware of midsemester
check-ins, but this unexpected
visit could only be a response
to something else unexpected;
since I was a runaway
minor who'd had her
granny forge her father's
signature, I had a feeling
I knew where this was going.
I'd never played poker;
was a Yahtzee face as effective?

"Iza," my advisor greeted me,
"typically I don't bombard
students during their work-studies

but I need to speak with you.
I just had a very *energetic*
interaction with your mother.
I'm gathering your divorced parents
aren't in agreement about
your transfer to Everleigh?"

I swallowed hard.
"That's correct."

"Is there anything *else* I need to know?"
"No, ma'am."
She studied me,
clearly not convinced,
but not pressed to push
me either.

"Very well," she conceded,
"but bear in mind, Ms. Jones,
raw talent is but a fraction
of what you'll need
to make it in the world.
We'll connect in a few
weeks to see how you're
fairing."

With my interrogation done,
all that was left was a
curt nod and dismissive
wave of her hand as she
left.

I let a sigh hiss out slow
and steady, willing
a calmness to settle
rather than the
panic that felt
like it was rooting
deep down into
my very core.

Mrs. Sullivan found me,
guided me through
her expectations
and my duties,
but I only half listened.
I couldn't shake these feelings:
like Icarus, I'd flown too close to the sun,
like Narcissus, I'd been fooled by a fantasy,
like Atlas, I'd be punished for daring to dream.

Apollo caught my gaze
from across the room
and I realized he'd realized it too.

27

By the time
we got to dinner
the hall was packed.
Apollo waited patiently
as I loaded my taco salad
into a haystack of more
toppings than lettuce.
I grabbed a bag of Doritos too:
the underrated Tex-Mex crouton.

Artie was sitting in the middle
of a full circular booth,
surrounded by new friends.
In fact, there wasn't a
free table in sight.
I was scanning the room for a
wall or ledge to lean on
and just shovel my dinner
when I heard a quick whistle
and my name.
Apollo had found a
table for two.

I scurried to him,
stomach grumbling,
urging me to pick up the pace.

I could feel his eyes
on me, studying me
or perhaps waiting
for an opening to ask
me what the hell
was going on
(he had to be wondering)
but the only sound
from Apollo was his
polite muffled chewing
as he took ungentlemanly
large bites of a meatball sub.

I crinkled my Doritos,
crunching the chips within
the bag before opening it.

Apollo's head bobbed approvingly,
"I'd wondered about that," he said,
motioning towards the Doritos.
"I'll have to try that."

"Trust," I said, a wise sage
of gestation snacks, "it'll
change your life."

His eyes twinkled as he took
another enormous bite
and I felt suddenly
overwhelmingly grateful
for our unexpected friendship
and began to ramble,
confessing everything I knew,
a few feelings tumbling
out that hadn't even been
a conscious thought yet:
I was fearful my best
wouldn't be,
couldn't be,

            enough.

Apollo must've been
a musician in another life
because he didn't miss a beat.
"You're enough, Iza,
if violin doesn't work out,
something else is meant for you,
believe that."

But what else was there? I thought
and as if he read my mind
Apollo said, "We'll figure it out."
Then he smirked,
grabbing an extra fork
(as if his intent was premeditated)
and commandeering a generous
bite of my taco salad.
He moaned, sitting back in the seat
as he set the fork back down,
"Damn," he purred like
a happy fat cat.
"Do you want me
 to make you one?"
I swear little hearts
booped into his eyes
and that was the moment
—if I believed in such things—
that Apollo fell in love.

28

Apollo walked me back.
It was a slow stroll after his
meatball-sub-taco-salad feast,
but that meant getting to
listen to him talk
about his day;
which ironically was
just as eventful as mine
but mildly less
traumatic, or perhaps
Apollo was just *that* fearless.

Artie found us
standing at our door,
just minutes before curfew,
laughing at Apollo's impression
of his professor mocking
him for a typo in his short story draft.
She squinted at us,
"This is giving serious
first-date-falling-in-like vibes."
I blushed, wordlessly pushing
past her in the doorway,
the sound of Apollo scolding

his twin trailing behind me.

But the powers that be
were offering no reprieves
for me: my phone began ringing
and to my horror **MOM**
blinked onto the screen.
        Foolishly I answered.

Mom was drunk (not like her),
and very angry (very much like her),
screaming horrible things, both
heard and never heard
by me before and I couldn't
breathe, let alone speak.

I looked away from the screen,
catching worried glances
from Artie and Apollo and
I just couldn't be that girl;
not today.

I ran to the bathroom,
bolting in quickly
with the intention of
locking the door

but Apollo was already
there, easing his way in
before the door
became a wall.

His hand on my back
had me on the brink
of crumbling.
It was hard to be
tough when someone
was kind;
at least when Apollo
was that someone.

"Hang up the phone,"
he encouraged softly.
"You do not deserve
nor should you allow
anyone to speak
to you like that."

I held my cell,
thumb hovering above
end call;
I knew I could
but I still felt like I couldn't.

"She'll just call back,"
I muttered, justifying
not standing up for myself.

Apollo rubbed my back
assuring and shrugged.
"Then block her calls
until you're ready to
talk to her. We're far
more than the sum
of our parents,
expectations and
disappointments
included!"

"Not me," I whispered,
"I did everything I
could and it's still
not enough because
deep down I know
I'm a coward."

"SAY SOMETHING, IZA!"
blared my mother's
voice through the
phone speaker.

"YOUR MOTHER
EXPECTS AN ANSWER."

Now, my mind screamed,
*do it now or she'll own you
for the rest of your days.*

I ended the call,
furiously scrolling
to my contacts to
block her number.
I didn't have to prove
anything to her.
I'd proved everything
already to myself.
I wasn't a child anymore
and she wasn't a mother.

I felt like I'd run a
marathon—I hadn't realized
how much energy
it took to be passive
and appease someone.
It was a hard habit to
break but it was done
and I could keep it *done*.

My legs felt mushy and
as Apollo pulled me
close. I realized I'd
sunk to the floor,
and as we leaned
against the bathroom
door together
I learned:
      true friends stay
      through the storms.

"You're not a coward, Iza Jones,"
Apollo said as he held me tight,
"you're the bravest person I know."

29

Hours to days,
days to weeks,
the first few flew
until I felt
like the living dead,
sledging through routines,
never
     really
          present.
I started to realize
you can't shake off
a funk when it's
depression.

30

I ran my hands over
the spines of books
I hadn't read yet.
The quiet library
with soft white noise
of clicking keys or
chair scooting or
whispers between
friends over
opened books
was soothing to me;
such a stark difference
from everything else.

On top of how hard
being on my own was,
the hardest part was
the call from my mother.
Usually I'd bottle,
but I couldn't stuff
it all down this time.

I'd begun sifting through,
sifted through emotions

by writing
        journal entries,
        and free verse poems
        and an odd little
        microfiction piece.
I wasn't sure why
I was writing, but the
words *had* to be written.

My ground felt unstable,
waving as my confidence
ebbed and flowed.
I was keeping up
with my nonmusic studies
and I'd even felt better
about the torture formerly
known as sight singing,
but I wasn't improving,
(and wasn't continuous
growth the true marker
of success?)
at least not the pace
I felt I should, the pace
I suspected was expected.

Lana made good on

her offer and brought
in the most beautiful
violin I'd ever held,
but she became ruthless
in her determination
to mold her student.

She didn't care about *me*,
just the music, as if
her investment in me
amplified her expectations,
as if not meeting them
was a poor return on
her educational dividend.

Artie was thriving.
We'd go to the dungeons
and I'd lean against the
adjoining wall
listening to her play
when I should be too
but was reading a book.

—buzz, buzz—
My phone brought me out of
reminiscing and back to reality.

Tiara calling.
Shit, I'd dodged her for weeks,
I hadn't read her texts or returned her calls.
I'd meant to follow up the same day
she'd started reaching out but
after my mommy drama
I'd been too deep in my own
problems to think about anyone else.

I answered before it could go to voicemail.
"Jesus, finally, where have you been?"
Tiara sounded more than stressed,
the tones of her voice
 spun in a panicked swirl.

"I'm sorry, I've just been busy.
What's going on? Are you alright?"

There was a pause,
a muffled sniffle, and finally,
"Can I stay with you?"
Tiara whispered.

I looked around
making sure no one
was near, could hear,

and then pushed deeper
between the rows of books.

"You can't stay with me," I whispered,
 "I'm at school, not a resort."

"I know, I know, I got into
a fight with my parents.
I can't go back. I just can't," Tiara insisted.

"Of course you can go back!"

"I've been out here since I dropped you
off Iza," Tiara started crying.
"What? Where are you?"
"I was in my car. I thought I could find a
job, you know like you did, but I can't.
I went to a shelter and they've been helping
but I'm so scared, Iza, I'm pregnant and I
don't know what to do. Dad won't even
look at me, Mom wants me to get rid
of it but it's not an *it* and I can't do it.
She says *she can make me,*
because I'm a minor, you know?
I don't know what to do."

I didn't know either, but I
had to say something.
I owed Tiara at least that.
"You'll be eighteen soon;
no one's making you do anything.
She's just upset and scared.
She loves you and she knows how
life changing having a baby is;
call your mom and go home, Tiara."

Tiara let out a nervous laugh,
"You're right, Iza. You're right."

"You'll work it out, you'll see."
"Did you and your mom?" Tiara asked.
I knew what she wanted to hear,
reassurance that she could
translate to her own story
but these days,
I couldn't stomach lying.

"No, we didn't, but we're
not you and your mom.
Trust me. It'll work out.
You'll see."

I hoped I was right
and I hadn't just sent
Tiara into a lion's den.

31

"I need to borrow Iza,"
I heard Apollo tell Mrs. Sullivan
a short while later.

"You need to *borrow* her?"
Mrs. Sullivan asked
skeptically.

"That's right," Apollo insisted.
I peeked between the books
and watched the ensuing
stare down, neither blinking,
neither moving to draw,
it would be till the death,
or perhaps would have,
until Mrs. Sullivan shrugged.

"Fine," she conceded.
"Iza has been sad lately,
really mopey, and with only an
hour left in her shift—why not?
Go cheer her up but don't
break too many rules."

Apollo looked offended.
"We're *friends*," he insisted,
honestly, a little too much
emphasis for my liking;
if anything he'd be
friend-zoned by me,
not the other way around.

I realized I'd blanked out
and shouldn't be peeking
through the transgressive
fiction section like some
American Psycho.

I should be fake-working
so I could act surprised
when Apollo found me.
Yeah, that was normal
teenage shit.

"Let's go, Iza Jones!"
I jumped at his voice
which made me snort
because I'd literally
just had an entire

inner monologue
about how I knew he
was headed my way.
Brains: can't live without 'em,
          can't think with 'em.

"Your shift is ending early
and we've got someplace to be."
"Who's we?" I quipped, "You
and the turd in your pocket?"
Apollo grinned; I laughed.
"Well played," Apollo said.
"Walked right into that," I pointed out.

"Seriously, Iza, you've been
struggling with *everything*
and sometimes you just have
to step back, take a break."

Knowing someone cared
didn't stop me feeling offended;
it stung that not only did I suck
but I couldn't even hide
it from everyone else.

He sighed, "However you took that
was not how I meant it."
Apollo moved closer
and placed my hand in his.
He held mine, so natural,
but beyond friendly,
making me feel like we
should never let go.

"You win. Let's go."
He grinned, giving my hand
a victorious tug to follow him
and we both knew I'd
succumbed to his charm,
but I was left wondering
when he'd started becoming
more than a friend.

32

Everleigh was set
in the middle area of
a downtown metropolitan,
meaning the edge
of campus met the city
and that border was
framed by public buildings:
    places to eat,
    places to drink,
    a library,
    a few museums,
    an art gallery or two
       and a planetarium;
a theater for the stars.

There'd been one in my
hometown called Longway;
nestled in our culture center,
a sacred place, a stark yin
from the yang of decaying
roads and buildings backdrop
of the inner city.
I hadn't been in years;
I'd never been to any other.

Nudging Apollo, I pointed
just ahead towards the
green domed building.
"We're going there,
aren't we?"

He feigned annoyance.
"Yes, you ruiner of surprises."

"Was I just supposed to
trust you to take me
on a magical journey
to an unknown destination?"
I teased.

"You were, but I'll forgive you
if you act surprised anyway.
At least I was right that you'd
like this sort of thing."
"I'm positively geeky
for galaxies," I assured him, "but you
didn't have to go out of your way for me."

"When it comes to you, Iza, I never mind."

Apollo switched from

playful to earnest
as if his feelings
were just below
the surface, waiting
for the right moment
between us
and I was overcome
with the feeling that
I didn't deserve an Apollo.

I tried to just
say thank you,
keep my tone light,
playful even,
but there was a bit of
self-loathing I couldn't
cleanse from my words.
I muttered,
"I don't know why you'd
go out of your way for me."

Apollo winked and reached for the
planetarium door. "You'll figure it out eventually."

He's into you Dum Dum sucker.
The realization was a heavy

wave, settling like a ton of
bricks on my mind.
I couldn't remember
anyone being into me
before. Had there been others
or was the difference here
that I maybe liked him too?

"Iza, did you just realize I want
to be more than friends?"

I internally gasped,
clutching figurative pearls
I wouldn't have worn
even if I'd owned some.
"I hate when you do that," I whispered.
"Hold doors for you?"
I smiled despite my inner rawr.
"Guess what I'm thinking," I said.
"You can't fault me for having a crush.
Ask any avid romance reader,
friends to lovers is a beloved trope."

He'd made a few good points,
but he won me over with the
way he was looking at me,

topping it off with a smile
I felt everywhere:
before the show while we
crunched astronaut ice cream,
during the show when our
arms brushed as we leaned
back to look at the stars,
and intensely after the show
when he asked me
if I'd had a good time.

33

During part two of our date,
Apollo said, "I need a favor,"
as we were stuffing our faces
with spuds at a
hole-in-the-wall spot called
Spuds whose entire menu was
various toppings stacked on
yam-sized baked potatoes.

It was glorious.

But not for the faint
of heart, as we had
only about an hour
before curfew; social
expectations for manners
were mashed as shoveling
ensued with wild *tubular* abandon.

"What's the favor?"
"Be my critique partner."
I almost choked on my toppings.
Apollo laughed, "Don't be surprised.
You read all the time; hell,

I wouldn't be surprised if
you could out write me."

"I've never written anything," I insisted.
Apollo activated his
reading-your-mind smolder.
"You know, the writing contest
is open to anyone," he said,
"despite your elected discipline."

Me writing seemed ridiculous;
I was a musician.
Everybody's got one,
singular talent—my gut flipped,
was music *not* mine?
I'd always been so sure.

"There are stages to the competition,"
Apollo went on. "The first round is
a pitch, the second is a sample,
and *when* we make it to the final,
you submit your entire manuscript."

"An entire novel?" I stammered.
"Not necessarily," Apollo said
between chews, "but it has to be

a fully thought-out concept,
whatever the format."

I was silent; my mind was loud.
I felt excited but the idea of doing
something only for myself,
trying something new,
doing something else instead
of what I should be
felt reckless, dangerous even.
There was a growing
part of me that didn't care.

Apollo reached across the table
and gave my hand a squeeze.
"It's okay not to be okay," he said,
"and it's also okay to change your
mind and try something new.
Besides, it's an excuse to spend
more time with your crush."

"You're the one with the crush."
I smiled and blushed and smirked
like an idiot going through the
whole colorful verb chart.

I realized we were
still holding hands;
palms sweaty,
arms weak and heavy,
thank god I hadn't eaten
anybody's mom's spaghetti.

Apollo released my hand
and checked his phone.
"Just think about it, Iza.
Shit, we gotta hurry up,
we can't be late and
I can't move fast when
I'm this full."

I almost clarified
exactly what
I was supposed
to be thinking about.

34

I got back just in time
for curfew and for Artie
to raise an eyebrow.

"I wondered where
you were," she said,
swiveling her desk chair
towards me. "You've seen Apollo
more than I have lately."

"He says he has a crush
on me," I blurted out.
"And what about you?"
Artie asked.
"We're really good friends."

Artie frowned,
she didn't believe me.

"Don't be upset with me—"
"It's not that," Artie interrupted,
"Apollo *likes* you. I've never
seen him act this way with
anyone. I know we haven't known

you long—it's been what, two months?—
but that's also like a million years.
Just don't break his heart or
I'll break your face."

My mouth dropped,
creating a vacuum that
voided the room of all
breathable air.

"Don't look so shook,"
Artie said, a bit more playful,
but still meaning absolute business.
"He's my twin; you shouldn't
expect anything less from me."

"It's not that I don't like him,"
I stuttered, my vernacular
faltering under that piercing,
no-bullshit gaze. "I've just only
had room for one thing in my life: violin."

"You've never dated anyone?"

I shook my head and the confession
momentarily deflated some of

Artie's protective sister gusto.
"All I meant," Artie said, sighing, "is that it's okay
for you to be with Apollo, but don't fuck
with his heart. No one deserves that."

"He thinks I should write," I blurted out.
"That I should enter a writing contest."
"Why not?"
"I have to get into an affiliate college
or coming to Everleigh was a waste," I said.
"Reading in the dungeons isn't exactly
productive."
She had me there.
"Just try it," Artie encouraged, "you never know
what you'll be good at.

"Just like that? Stop playing and start writing?"

"Well not *just* like that," Artie said.
"You'll have to get your counselor
sign off, but if you're going to
pivot, first semester is your best shot.
Get recognition in that contest;
that'll get you a lot of clout.
Until you know for sure, juggle both."

I was frightened
by how hopeful I felt;
it made me realize
how unhappy I was.
It was the one thing I hadn't planned for.

35

It's no surprise that
I couldn't sleep.
I wasn't too worried;
Fridays were a relaxed,
music-free day.

I gave up; giving in instead
to the black hole scroll of the internet,
drowning in dopamine,
watching funny dog videos.

My email icon blinked
with a notification that
Apollo had emailed me.

Of course, I opened it right away.

Here's a link to
the writing contest submission
page. There are three categories:
Hughes for poetry,
Angelo for literary fiction,
Butler for genre writing
(specifically sci-fiction, paranormal).

I wasn't encouraging you
just because I like you. I see
the way you look at books.
You've got a writer's soul.
Writing is something anyone can do
but a few (like you) can be extraordinary.
Plus, there's something magical
writers have that musicians do not;
the ability to revise their work.
Just give it a chance.

-Apollo

I could feel how
flushed my cheeks were;
if an email was making me blush,
I shouldn't deny it
was due to having a crush,
but I only felt safe admitting that
in an inner monologue
no one could quote.

I clicked the attached pdf,
skimmed the basic rules;
it was just like Apollo had said,
but he hadn't mentioned the

deadline was in three days.

There wasn't time
to weigh my options;
if I wanted it,
I'd have to leap
and pray I could fly.

36

I decided to go see my
advisor, but without
an appointment it felt
more like an ambush.

I couldn't stop thinking
about writing. I'd even
dreamed about it
the night before;
I'd had a noir fantasy,
all smoke and haze,
where my fingers
plucked away on a
mechanical keyboard,
so sure of each word
and the next after it
that I couldn't make
a mistake. I bled
onto the page,
freely giving everything;
and for once it was enough.

I'd never felt that
with violin—and

who knows if I'd feel
that way writing—but
the lure was strong
and I was hooked
securely enough to
feel in my gut I had
to try, and that meant
talking to my advisor.

I had to know if
this fever dream
could be real,
because the one thing
I wouldn't accept was
leaving Everleigh with *nothing*.

Finding her office
was easy enough
but as I leaned forward
to knock, the door opened
on its own; I was
face to face with Lana.

"Iza!" she chirped,
"your ears must have
been burning."

I grimaced—there was no
way that was a good thing
coming from her.

"Practice hard this weekend.
We're going to have a
heart-to-heart on Monday,
'a real talk, no cap' as the
kids say." Lana laughed,
as if she really believed she
was witty. Patting me on the
shoulder she offered a final
worthless anecdote, "Music is hard,
> even for a prodigy,
> but one thing we all
> have in common is that
> we must want it badly
> enough to dig deep
> and make it happen.
> You have to *make* it happen, Iza;
> you won't just wake up better,
> you have to *make* yourself better."

With a shoulder squeeze
and a condescending nod,
she was gone.

"Have a seat," my advisor
said, motioning to the
chair adjacent to her desk.

"Professor Grande isn't always
tactful but I imagine the reasons
you both have for seeing me are the same.
Tell me what's on your mind, Iza."

I let it all out,
letting the office
fill with feelings until
instead of me on the
brink of bursting
it was the room.

"You've got a tenacious
spirit and as cliché as it sounds
you really can do anything
you set your mind to;
but you must *set* your mind
and stick to it.
Do you understand?"

"Switching my focus from music
 to writing isn't an option?"

"No," she said, "but unlike
other students, you have
one year to get from *here*
to an affiliated university;
you don't have the liberty
of changing your mind
more than once."

"But how can I know
what I don't know?" I
said, feeling exasperated.

"Can I be direct?"

I nodded.

"Figure out your shit,
Iza, it's just that simple.
If you want to be a
writer, be a writer but
don't squander opportunities.
Gobble up everything you can,
take it all, because
these kind of opportunities
are rare."

"I'm going to write
the pitch and if I make it
to round two I'll switch
course directions."

She smiled approvingly.
"Good, keep me apprised
of your progress and, Iza,
I'm glad you came to me.
I am on your side."

Maybe she was,
maybe she wasn't,
it didn't matter either way;
I was going to make it,
no matter what.

37

"Try to convince me,"
Artie teased, "that you
came bowling with me
and my friends for
me and my friends
and not just to make
swoony-googly-heart eyes
at my brother all night."

I heard her, (even
over the clanking pins
and throwback jams)
I swear I did, it was just the
way Apollo walked up to the lane,
the way his (surprisingly toned)
arm flexed as he threw the ball,
the way he danced,
when he scored a strike
or a spare, his confidence
was more than sexy;
it was mesmerizing.

A hand playfully slapped
my arm and I was jerked

back from my thoughts
to the reality that I hadn't
been paying attention to
a word Artie had said.

"Iza Jones," she scolded,
"you really took my
'you can like my brother'
speech to heart. You're not
even *pretending* to listen to me."

"What speech did who take to heart?"
Apollo appeared smugly smirking
as if he knew exactly what or
rather who we'd been talking about.

"Where exactly are your friends?
It's just been us the whole time,"
I teased Artie.

"I only invited one new friend,
but the only way he's staying
just a friend, is if he zones himself."

Apollo scowled. "Do I know him?"
Artie scowled harder. "Don't you even start."

But he did start, and they easily slipped into
bickering like siblings on a '90s sitcom.
It was adorable until they forgot
I was sitting right there.

"I didn't whine when you started
schmoozing my best friend," Artie snapped.
"She's also my friend," Apollo countered.
"I'm your best friend?" I squeaked.
They twinned; turning in unison to yell *yes*.
Aw, admittedly, I was touched.

"Show up a little late and
you'll miss all the fun," said a deep,
far too suave voice.

Artie blushed as she turned around,
quickly finding herself entangled
in her "friend's" arms.
They were so close and gazing so intently
into each other's eyes that I was disappointed
when all that happened was a hug.

"We'll be back," Artie called over
her shoulder. Her still nameless friend
laughed, letting her lead him away

towards the concession counter.

"It's your turn, Art," Apollo called teasingly.
"Play for me," she replied, without
even looking at the scoreboard.
It was definitely *my* turn, not hers.

"Do you know who he is?" Apollo asked.
"A theater tech kid, I think?"
Apollo scowled.
"A thespian?"
"Is there a geek hierarchy I'm unaware of?"
He laughed.
"It's just weird when it's your sister.
Got plans for this weekend, Iza?"

"Just writing."
Apollo's face lit up. "Seriously?"
"Seriously," I echoed.
"Then you do have plans because
we're having a writing party."

38

Saturday afternoon, Artie
fell like a flapjack on to
her duvet, with a happy sound
closer to a sing than a sigh.

"He's on his way over,"
she declared, and I knew
he was Arnold the handsome
devil we'd briefly met
at Pete's Pins last night.

I thought they were cute,
Apollo seemed unsure
but tolerant long as
Artie was happy.
It was a fun night for me,
with Apollo so jarred
off his game, I won
every single time.

"Have I told you how we met?"
Artie asked and then launched
into their origin story before I could
remind her that yes, she had in fact

told me three times now.
I didn't mind.

"I signed up for the
theater pit orchestra—
they're doing *Wicked* this
year and it sounded fun.
I never realized
how few people take
an interest in the techy
side and Arnold is a
genius with his hands.
I'm learning a lot."

"I bet you are," I teased.

"Yeah, yeah, yeah, I walked
into that," Artie said bashfully.
"But seriously, he can do everything
from electrical to carpentry to–"

"Should he," I interjected, "be doing electrical?"

"Probably not, but his mom is a
master electrician—what a boss,
I can't even imagine working

in such a male-dominated field.
It's not going to be weird, is it?
The three of us hanging out?"

"Not at all," I said. "I have
plans with Apollo."
Artie, Apollo, Arnold…
There sure were a lot of
A-named folks in my life.

"He's so into you," Artie said,
"and I'm here for it, but
not the details because that'd
be super cringe. In case you
were wondering, you do
have my blessing though."

I smiled. "I knowingly
accept the conditions
of your blessing. I'm just
a little unsure of how
this all works. The last
'boyfriend' I had I
checked a 'yes' box on a
note that my friend
had pretended he wrote

when really *she* had."

Artie laughed so hard
I thought she might roll
off her bed.

"Iza, that doesn't count
and also I'm not going to
help you charm my
baby brother."

"You're twins…"
"Don't argue, I was born
first, it's documented
and therefore I'm older.
But seriously, Iza, just go with
it. You'll know all the things you
need to know when you need to
know them."

"I need more friends," I grumbled.

Artie held up a hand in protest.
"Quality over quantity, Iza,
get some standards!"

39

Iza: When does the writing party start?
Apollo: new phone, who this?

I chewed my cheek
in a panic wondering
what the odds were
that Artie would give
me a fake number.

BING. BING.

Apollo: It's me but
you never asked me
for my number so I had
to get my revenge.
Apollo: now the party don't
start till I walk in.
Me: I'd never have guessed
you were a Kesha fan.
Apollo: Don't fence me in!
Me: Now, Labyrinth is right up your alley.
Apollo: Still thinking about last night…
Me: Of course, I've never been so victorious.
Apollo: Victorious at losing?

Me: I won.

Apollo: Not without Artie's generous handicap.

Me: That was one game.

Apollo: One game that wasn't *won.*

Apollo: Can you come over in an hour?

Me: I don't know *can* I?

Apollo: I have snacks.

Me: On my way.

"Jesus," Artie yelled from
the bathroom where she was
primping in a hurry, "either put your
phone on silent or just call him."

40

I'd never been to
Apollo's room before,
he always came to ours.
His was cleaner than I'd expected,
although tiny living
didn't allow for much clutter;
unless you thrived on chaos.

"Beanbag, bed or desk?"
Apollo offered chivalrously.
I weighed the options:
 the bed, absolutely not;
 his desk, felt invasive;
 bean bag, optimal choice.
"The beanbag is fine."

He smirked and then dug
on the side of his bed
hidden from my sight
and produced two
beanbags and lobbed
them over to where I stood.

I raised an eyebrow accusingly.
"You've *done* this before…"

But my teasing left him unfazed.
"Of course I have," he said
with a shrug, "many a girl
has been seduced on these
beanbags, but you're the prettiest."

I mocked barf sounds
and he nearly toppled
over with laughter.
The good kind,
so free and genuine
it almost wasn't attractive,
but it was because you
knew he only laughed
that way for people
he let in.
      Girls ugly cry,
      boys ugly laugh.

Nestled down into our cozy
expanded polystyrene beans,
we both queued up

our preferred music
and got to work.

I snuck peeks at Apollo;
he was *focused*,
occasionally unconsciously
half smiling as he wrote,
confident enough not to
take himself too seriously.

I focused back on my own
blank screen; unsure of
where to start, so I just *did*.

With a deep breath, I let go,
writing whatever came,
it was just me and the page;
no one to judge.

41

IDEAS

#1

Two zombies discover each other
when their hunting grounds
unintentionally cross.
It could have been a disaster,
but it turns into a friendship
neither of them expected.
Maybe they are coworkers? Could be fun.

#2

Story begins with a woman running
from a monster we never see, but
does catch her and ultimately she dies.
We jump to the woman
waking up, reborn,
in another plane of existence.
But what are the stakes?
The planet is inhabited by
two main races on the brink of war
and whether right or wrong,
the side she belongs to is already chosen.
Would it be too much if they survive on

just water and sex? Like a chiller,
consensual, mutual succubus vibe?

I paused, pondering my ideas;
they felt a little out there.
Yet, I didn't feel discouraged,
honestly, I was excited;
if these books existed I'd read them,
but they weren't the expected content
for a high school student.

I took another slow breath
and started again.

#3

After a traumatic event,
a girl runs out of a local business
and into another alternative reality
where she is believed to be
a prophesied messiah
destined to prevent a civil war.

I gasped, giggled, guffawed!

Apollo grinned.

"Are you having a stroke?" he asked.

"I have a good idea!"

"That's great, Iza," Apollo said, "keep writing."

"Don't you want to–

"Nope, no influences, just Iza."

Right! I had to do this on my own.

42

We took a break around seven,
Apollo convincing me
to try Thai food (delicious)
and then we hit up the campus
gas store for frozen cokes
and assorted snacks.
If this had been a date
it would have been *perfect*.

"Does this count as a date?"
Apollo casually asked as if he
could read my mind;
making me choke on my coke,
nearly squirting it out my nose.
"Jesus," he said solemnly, "if you
don't like me, just say so."

"No, no," I insisted, "it's just,
sometimes you say things I'm
thinking and it freaks me out."

"So this *does* count as a date."
I clanked our frozen cokes.

"You did pay for everything."
Apollo grinned. "That was very
date-like of me, wasn't it?"
"I'll allow it," I teased.

We walked back in silence.
I'm sure both of us wondered
what the other was thinking
but also not wanting to
break this comfortable
feeling between us,
that had settled into a
familiarity that was just *us*.

He was right, I thought,
with a romantic flair fueled
by all the food and sugar
I'd ingested in the past hour,
friends to lovers was a beloved trope.

"Iza," Apollo began hesitantly,
"you know I don't just like you,
I care about you, and I can't stop
thinking about you and I'm so
thankful you're so clumsy you

smacked into me that day
because I can't imagine a world
where I don't know you."

"You bumped into me," I corrected,
"I feel the same way you do."
Apollo shifted the snack bag
and took my hand in his.

43

Neither of us wanted the
night to end, and since
Apollo's roommate was
gone for the weekend,
it didn't seem like it had to;
so we plopped on his bed,
binging *Law & Order*
(*Special Victims Unit*, of course)
and kept working on our writing.

I'd submitted my pitch already,
now I was outlining.
I'd even drafted a chapter,
and why not? I was on fire,
I was committed to optimism,
and when my pitch got accepted
I was going to be *ready*.

Eventually we dug into our snacks,
pairing perfectly with our
only-funny-to-us
commentary as we watched
Olivia and Elliot do their thang,
and the night got later and later

as our dorm curfew flew past.
Neither of us mentioned it
because we didn't care,
not to mention, logically,
it was smarter to stay than leave
and get caught walking around
campus late at night.

When it was technically
tomorrow, Apollo made us
spicy ramen bowls and we
switched from *SVU* to classic.
I don't know when I fell
asleep but when
I woke up I was startled
to find myself sprawled
atop lightly snoring Apollo.

44

All the carb-fueled confidence
was gone in the daylight;
what remained was my mind zipping
through various scenarios and outcomes
spanning from, *did I drool on him*, to
could we get expelled for this?
Apollo's arms tightened around
my waist and he brushed a
reassuring kiss against my brow.

"It's too early for you
to be thinking that loudly," Apollo
murmured. "We won't make
sleepovers a regular thing
until college, I promise."

I leaned back to look at him
and he smirked at the feel
of me shifting in the bed
but didn't open his eyes.

"Don't gawk at me, Iza Jones," he teased,
"you're my girlfriend, not my mother."

The nerve; I jabbed him
in the side for that sass
and he laughed in surprise.
Apollo yawned with a
big feline-like stretch
before scurrying off
to the bathroom.

As I began to wake up
and get my bearings, my
anxiety subsided replaced by
what-we-did-wasn't-so-bad logic;
we were both fully dressed,
nothing had happened,
and it had never been a crime
to fall asleep.
It was fine, everything was fine.
Did he just call me his girlfriend?

45

I opened my dorm door to
a screeching Artie,
the flash of buns,
and the slamming shut
of a bathroom door.

Arnold stretched,
casually pulling
a T-shirt over his head
before scooping his
pants up off the floor.

"Good morning," he said smugly.
I peeked over my shoulder
to find him fully clothed,
gathering Artie's clothes
as he strode to tap
on our bathroom door.

"Art," he said coyly,
winking at me, "crack the door."
She did, and he immediately stuck
his face through to kiss her,

causing an array of giddy giggles
before finally handing over her clothes.

Arnold didn't dally;
when the bathroom door
reopened he was long gone.

Artie emerged, flushed face and high spirits.
"Don't say *anything*," she said.
"What can I say? I just got back myself."
"That's why I said 'don't say anything.'
I don't want to hear any gritty details unless
Apollo was a jerk, then I'll destroy him."

"He was the opposite of a jerk."
Artie sighed. "Good! You can assume
but you never really know, and I'd hate to
have to make myself an only child."

"So," I said, ready for tea,
"just because you don't want
to hear about my night doesn't mean I
don't want to hear about yours."

"Guuuurl," Artie sang,
turning with a look that said it all.

46

The rest of Sunday
was relaxed; Artie and I gossiped,
eventually going to the dungeons
to practice but I'd brought my laptop instead.

Tik, tok,
Monday morning I wake up
feeling like Kesha,
grab my glasses,
I'm out the dorm;
I'm gonna hit these classes.
Okay, not really, but I did feel refreshed.

It wasn't until I
was gathering
what I'd need for
classes when it dawned
on me: I hadn't played
violin all weekend.

I was stunned,
the definition of
flabbergasted incarnate.
I played every day;

obviously I'd skipped Sunday,
being wrapped up in writing,
but I'd forgotten I hadn't played
Friday or Saturday either.
It was rare for me to skip,
but even rarer for me to miss
days in a row.

"What's wrong?" Artie asked
from her desk.
"I didn't play once this weekend."
"I took it light too, just Sunday, glorious right?"

She was right—it'd been magnificent.

"That's why you're not
'improving,'" Artie theorized.
"Music isn't fun anymore.
If you lose your why,
then you get off course.
What's your *why*?"

"My reason for playing?"
Artie nodded.
"To get into Everleigh," I said.
Artie tsked disapprovingly.

"That's the problem right there,
your why is past its sell-by date.
You need a new one."

47

Class with Lana (later) was
a cold shock to the system.
She was livid with me,
my relaxed energy triggered
her Spidey senses:
her gut had informed
her that I hadn't practiced.

Lana the merciless tyrant,
criticizing my inability to hear
that my D string was flat,
chastising me for using a tuner
and then doubling down
disgusted that I'd contradict her
when I showed her the
sound reading was perfectly
centered, meaning:
the string was in tune;
I should be able to *feel*
when it's right.

It went on and on
      you're not using your full bow,
      your wrist looks *weak,*

your sound isn't robust,
your phrasing lacks emotion,
your thumb *isn't* bent.

At one point, the traditional lesson
stopped and Lana insisted I
do a hundred bow strokes
hitting a duct-taped **X** on a wall,
to learn what a straight arm
and a full bow stroke
felt like.

Next we focused on my bow grip,
Lana held her hand above my
perpendicular bow, while I flexed
the bow (without moving my arm)
to tap the bow tip into her hand.

Finally, when I thought we'd
use the remaining scrap of time
to work on my solo, she handed
me a green book of études,
music focused on
technique and form.

"You're a natural artist

in a lot of ways, Iza,"
Lana lectured with grandiose
wisdom, "but there's no denying
your progress has plateaued;
your lack of technique,
and knowledge has
stunted your growth.

These are things learned
at the beginning;
to learn them now
will be hard, but not impossible;
we're going to strip you down to basics."

I nodded hesitantly, not
sure I wanted to know where
this conversation was headed.

"No more vibrato. I want you
to focus on the sound
and intonation of each note."

"Even when I'm playing
a concerto?" I asked.

"You won't be playing

any concertos, just études
and scales."

"What about my jury," I asked.
I knew full well what she wanted
wouldn't fly when I was judged by
Everleigh's music faculty.
There were strict requirements
in order to pass a jury.

"I'm not concerned about that.
I'm concerned about getting you
ready for college auditions."

A music jury
is a final performance
by a music student for a panel of
adjudicators, usually consisting
of faculty of the institution.

The definition was
textbook classic;
an unarguable rule;
an inescapable expectation;
but Lana didn't know
that, because she was a

prodigy.

I was plucked.

48

"She can't be serious," Apollo whispered.
"Like a heart attack," I muttered.

He grumbled inaudible words,
thumping another book
back in its spot as I
pushed the library cart
down the aisle.
Apollo had been helping
me in the back rows
of the library for an hour,
so he could hear me
complain about my
Lana-drama-trauma.

It was sweet,
and even though
I was still upset;
I wasn't *as* upset
as I would have been
if he wasn't here.

I felt…hashtag blessed.

Apollo eyed me.
I must have been
the evil queen,
snickering out loud
at her own inner monologue

"Is this a laugh so
we don't cry situation?"
"Totally," I confirmed.
"What are you going to do?"
"Well, my advisor won't even
consider switching me
unless I make it to the final
round of the writing contest.
For now, all I can do is wait."

"It's always been
so strange to me," Apollo
said, "that the expectation
has always been for us to
know now what we'll want
in twenty years from now.
There's little room for growth."

I sighed in
silent agreement.

I'd been thinking
about that a lot too;
how many of my choices
were made out of
frantic desperation.
If I'd been able to
slow down and try things
would I have picked
another route?
Or was it inevitable
that the grass was
always greener,
and your heart
never meant for
contented happiness?

—buzz, buzz—
My phone twitched in my
pocket, fingers slipping as
I scrambled to get it out.
Why did the sound of
a vibrating phone feel
so loud in a quiet place?

I had a new email from
the writing department.

It said a lot but all I saw was:

Your pitch has been accepted.

49

Writing Contest, Second Round
Submit the first 15K words of your pitched
manuscript.

Title: Unnatural
Writer: Iza Jones
Genre: Young Adult/Urban Fantasy
Summary: After a traumatic event,
a girl runs out of a local business
and into an alternative reality
where she is believed to be
a prophesied messiah destined
to prevent a civil war.

I tapped my foot
in angry triplets,
leaning against our
old oak door as I
complained impatiently,
"Everything will be gone
before we get there."

"I'm coming," my mom called.
"Just need to grab my lipstick."
"For what?" I whined.
"Don't rush me,"
she snapped back and
I groaned in annoyance;
it was definitely
going to be a while.

Every Thursday night
we walked the handful
of blocks down to our
corner store,
the Lucky Lizard Liquor;
it was our weekend eve
ritual (we got snacks and
watched a movie
we'd already seen) but
all of this pruning,
hair fluffin' and fussin',
was because my mom
had a thing with the
store owner, Darrell.
Seriously—all this drama
was for ten minutes of flirting
and a bag of snacks.

Eighty-four years later
we were at the store,
door chiming as we entered,
Darrell whooping an
enthusiastic greeting to my mom.
"You look so pretty tonight," he crooned,
and her lashes fluttered so hard
they created a breeze through
the candy aisle.
With a matching purple jacket
to her purple jeans,
I'm sure she was fine as hell
to Darrell, you know, being they
were geriatric colleagues and all.

I'd moved to the back
of the store, mulling over
what combination of two-for-one
candy I should get, when I heard
the bell chirp again.

The energy of the room chilled
and I looked up.
A figure dressed in black
swept across the tiles
until he was centered

square to the cash register.
Darrell saw him first
(being faced that way)
and his startled expression
caused my mother to
turn around. At the same
time the figure's hand stretched
outward.

"Don't point that gun at me!"
she shrieked in surprise.
"I'm the one giving orders!"
the man spat back.
"Get down on the floor,
hands out, don't move!"

I got down too,
crouching as low
as I could; looking
for anything I could
use as a weapon as
I heard the robber
instruct Darrell to give him
everything in the register.

But he hesitated to comply.

"Do I know you?" Darrell asked.
"Your voice sounds familiar;
maybe we can work something out."

This only agitated the man more.
My eyes darted to my mother's;
she was lying on the ground,
stomach down, but looking directly
at me mouthing "go" repeatedly.

How could I leave her?
The stress made me shake.
I'd never seen her,
so fearfully frantic,
so determined to save me
if nothing else.

The arguing between
the men intensified
and so did my mother's
urgent mouthed go;
inevitable events were
dawning.

I wanted to defy her,
to fight for our lives
but she was crying now

and her tears forced
my hand to be obedient.

I twisted around
finding an emergency
exit behind me at the
opposite end of the aisle.
I could make it,
but once I made the move
there was no turning back.
I looked at my mother
hoping she'd changed her
mind but she hadn't.
Please go, she said wordlessly.
I took a deep, shaky breath,
and ran.

50

I'd been waiting
nervously for Apollo
to finish reading *Unnatural*.
"Don't tell Artie
I let you read it first," I
said anxiously.
He shushed me,
brow furrowing as
he tucked a page
to the back of the pile.

"It's okay if you don't like
it," I stammered.
He reached for my hand,
eyes never leaving the page
as if he knew exactly
where my hand would be.

Holding hands wasn't new;
usually it happened when
I was spiraling
and he was soothing,
or it was a quick
grab and release,

but this was different:
our fingers interlocked,
his thumb trailing
a path over mine;
my breath hitched in
my chest.

Absorbed in my work
he pulled me closer,
depositing my hand on his
thigh to stuff another page
to the back of the pile,
before resuming holding my
hand.

Are we gonna do a thing? Brain asked Heart.
Don't ask questions, Heart murmured back.

I scooted closer,
using the excuse
that I wanted to see
what he was reading
without disturbing him,
but the truth was
I just wanted to.

When my cheek grazed
his shoulder and he turned,
his unaware half smile
tugging into a full smirk.

"It's really good, Iza," he praised.
"I can't even imagine what it'll be
like when you revise it. You should
be proud. Very proud."

I knew the correct response
was *thank you* but I couldn't speak;
my eyes flitting between
his eyes and his lips
and then *his eyes*
were on my mouth too
and rom-com mode
was activated.

Only a breath
between us now;
he stayed so still,
his hand curved
around my forearm
in a way that felt intimate
when it shouldn't—

(how could such a
light touch feel so heavy?).
Apollo didn't move,
as if any shift might
scare me off
and snap us from this dream.
Apollo was waiting for me,
he'd always been
waiting for me.

I needed to kiss him,
and my head eased
in his direction then hesitated,
just a fraction before
our lips touched,
remembering that:
I'd never kissed anyone before.
　　What if he didn't like it?
What if I didn't like it?
　　What if I did it wrong?
What if I didn't even know
I'd done it wrong and that made it
extra wrong and he never
ever kissed me again?

Oh god, what if he *never*
kissed me again?

Apollo smirked,
and in less than a
millisecond,
I knew *he knew*
what I was thinking.
"Get out of your head,
Iza, and kiss me."
"I've never kissed anyone," I whispered.
"Me neither."
I gasped; he laughed at my gasp.
"Do you want to kiss me?" Apollo asked.
I nodded.
"Then *do it*."
His hand dragged up
the back of my arm,
his forehead pressed gently
against mine,
our lips so close
all I had to do was tilt
towards him, so I did.

Our kiss was softer
than I'd expected,

soap operas always
smashed faces together
in erratic abandon that
was hyped up to be
the best kiss
but *this*, Apollo's
slow exploration,
his hand at the nape
of my neck urging me closer
as we got increasingly
comfortable and a first kiss
became a third and a fourth;
his kiss was the best kiss.

"Get the *fuck* off my daughter!"
Like lightning struck,
we broke apart
and to my horror
in the doorway stood
my father.

Part Three

She will be plucked, they declared,
a slang phrase describing
a universal truth:
the house always wins.

51

> It is only a matter of time
> before a plucked flower
> withers and dies;
> but first it blooms.

The last time I'd seen
my father was at a concert.
I was twelve, just starting to feel
good at violin and the Seitz
concerto was my T-ball to
baseball, training wheels off,
portal to a new world,
and he'd heard me play
and then he felt confident
that I was doing fine without
him or a two-parent home
and he went back to his life
doing things he liked
with people he wanted to be
with more than his only
daughter.

And now,
he was back.

"Why are you here?"
I blurted out.
It was rude but I was
matching his energy
and it was easy
to justify it without a
second thought.

"I wanted to come
see the fancy prep school
I sent my daughter to,
a school so wonderful
that it was worth sending
my ex into a rage.
Then I come here,
expecting to hear
music emanating
down the hallways,
but instead I see
you acting like a
horny little slut—"

Apollo stood up
and moved in front
of me.

"Careful," Apollo warned,
his eyes burning with barely
checked aggression.
"I don't care who you are,
you're not talking to Iza like that."

"Is that so?" My father
sounded impressed
and he probably was;
no one stood up to him
(other than my granny).

I wanted to, but whenever
I was in his presence,
emotions overwhelmed me.
I couldn't get a full thought out,
and he knew that weakness well,
always ready to shut me down,
push me back in my place
with a carefully crafted sentence.

No. More.
I moved beside Apollo.
Chin up. Ready to fight for myself.

"Did you want something?"
I demanded.

"To see *you*! And what I saw
I didn't like. I didn't raise
you to act like this."

"You didn't raise me
and you're just upset
that I've flown without you.
So, I'll ask you again,
what do you want?"

He was speechless,
or dumbfounded,
or whatever other
adjective; it didn't
matter. I'd never let
him or my mother
take my voice away
again.

"I don't owe you an explanation.
I don't owe Mom an apology,
but I do owe myself
a chance to be happy in a

capacity that I actually want,
whether that's being a musician
or a writer,
or a horny little slut,
because it's my life.

So if you don't have
anything to say, shit,
even if you *do*, get
the fuck out before
I have you put the
the fuck out."

The cat really had
his tongue then.
All he could do
was leave.

52

My father slammed
the door behind him.
I crumbled
to the floor.

"I never talk to
anyone like that,"
I whispered. "I can
never take it back.
He's never going
to let me take it back."

Apollo sat down beside
me and pulled me into
his arms.

"I got you, Iza," he
said softly.

I cried and cried;
it was like mourning
it was grieving
for kid Iza,
and today's Iza,

for future Iza;
once I start really
feeling,
I can't just *stop*.
I'm a broken
jar with all
of me just
pouring
out.

53

Apollo stayed with me.
I didn't have to ask.
He just did.
He just knew.

He held me in
a tight hug
all night
as if he wanted
me to feel he
was there
even in my sleep.

At some point
in the night
I woke up
long enough to
murmur
"…don't get in trouble
because of me,"
and he just
held me tighter.

54

He was gone when I
woke up and I
felt confused
wondering if
it'd all been too much.

"Apollo is just getting
us breakfast," Artie said.
"He told me to remind you
to submit your story. It's
due today, right?"

Shit. It was due today.

I grabbed my laptop
off the nightstand
and rushed to the
contest forum.

"Iza," Artie said,
as I typed,
"What's going on?
Apollo wouldn't say."

I stared at my laptop
screen as I answered.

"My father has never
been around,
my mother resents me
but also needs me
and refused to let
me come to Everleigh
so my paternal grandma
forged my father's
signature and I got
a ride up here without
my parents knowing.
My mom called my dad
and he caught me kissing
Apollo and called me a slut."

"Holy shit," Artie cursed.
"What did he want?"
"No idea. I yelled at my dad
and made him leave."
"Are you okay?"
"No, but I will be."

I hit **submit**.

55

It took me almost a week
to work up the nerve
to call my mom.

I was anticipating
the turmoil of emotions
pooled between us
and I couldn't stop thinking
maybe there was no going back
leaving like I did had
also been leaving her
and she wouldn't forgive me
she'd want me to feel
how final going against her was.

Still, even knowing all of that,
I felt like I had to try,
so I took a deep, deep breath
and dialed.

   waiting
for
the
call

to

  connect

and then three little tone beeps
and then a *this number is no longer in service*
and then everything I'd known
became everything I had to accept,
she didn't consider me hers anymore.

56

I thought about skipping
my violin lessons
(I never should
have tried to
call my mom
an hour before)
but if the alternative
was sitting in an empty
dorm room or
hiding out in the library
it just didn't seem
to make sense.
I thought the routine,
the familiar feel
of the bow and strings
as the sound pooled
in the air around me
would help and maybe
it would have if I'd
been playing for myself
but I was playing for Lana.

"WRONG," she screeched.
Then put little pencil dots

all over a note I'd missed
"If you're not going to
play it right then don't
play at all."

I stared at her.
All my non-her related
emotions merged
with all the shit
she'd been putting
me through and I snapped.

"Fine," I said.
I placed the
violin and bow
back in the case,
the only sound
the zipper
as it sealed shut.

"What are you doing?"
"I'm done," I said.
Lana crossed her arms
and *smirked;* a look that
blared *is that so?*

"You've been riding
my ass since day one."

"More like day two," she
replied, "you had your shit
together on day one."

"Take your violin back."

She looked stunned as
if it just dawned on her
that I was really upset
and not just throwing a
tantrum for attention
or whatever incorrect
interpretation she'd had
that'd led her to indignantly
smirking in the first place.

"You can't quit," Lana said.
"Is this about your sudden
interest in writing? You can't
be serious. It's just a distraction."

"If you think just because you're
a professor and I'm a student

that I'm going to let you
berate me day in and out,
you're wrong. You know
how I know I can quit?
Because I just did."

"Like I told your advisor,
I'm not letting you *go*," Lana said.

"Why? Do you get off
on being cruel? You don't
even like me or think I'm
talented and I'm under
so much pressure
I don't even want to play.
This isn't what I want."

"Iza, wait," Lana said
her tone less haughty
and more vulnerable
and even though I had
one foot out the door,
I turned back around.

"I admit, I am an ass,
and I could work on that,

but I just see the talent,
I see the potential,
and can make you
extraordinary."

"I don't need to be molded,
I don't need to be extraordinary;
I need to fly."

"And you think
writing will give you
big enough wings
to fly you anywhere
worth going?" Lana quipped.

"It's better than staying here
and letting you pluck
me down to raw skin."

"Maybe you're right,
you did get into
the last round of
that writing contest—"

"How do you know
that," I gasped.

"The staff gossips. But
like I said, I won't let
you switch disciplines,
but if you want to
come to a truce and
start fresh then I'll
support you doing both."

"You don't have the right—"

"No, I have the power,"
Lana said, "look, my methods
are unconventional but
you're special Iza, and my
goal is to get you into
a great music program.
It'll change your life
and from what I've
pieced together from
looking into you,
you can't afford for this
to go wrong, can you?"

My eyes burned,
a mirroring emotion
to everything

I had felt,
hadn't felt,
all of it.

There wasn't anything
left to say because Lana,
monster that she was today,
was right and I knew what
I had to do.

I grabbed my violin and left.

57

I pulled each book
to the edge of the rack
one by one
working my way
shelf by shelf
until the rack was
perfect.

I heard the familiar
sound of footsteps
against the checkered
tiled floor and looked
up to see Apollo striding
towards me.

He pulled me into
his arms, his hands
tangling in the
hem of my T-shirt
as he held me tight.

"How are you?"
he murmured,

pulling back to
look at me.

I shrugged.
Talking about it
would lead to
crying about it
and I just didn't
even want to
think about it.

Apollo cupped
my cheeks in
his hands
searching my eyes
for what I wasn't
saying.

"I can stay
over again," he said.

"No, don't," I said
quickly.

He stiffened,
hands dropping back to

his sides and I couldn't
risk him not understanding;
I quickly grabbed his hands
pulling him back to me
a little too quickly
and we ended up
hip to hip
lips to lips
as we let our
emotions slide
into a moment
where I forgot
what I was even
upset about, and
when we finally
pulled back apart
I said, "I just
don't want either of us
to get kicked
out of Everleigh."

Apollo smirked,
eyes on my mouth
and replied, "Can
you tell me again,
maybe five more times?"

There was a cough
and I saw Mrs. Sullivan
saunter by.

Apollo winked
as he strode
away.

58

The repetitive *boop*
of the bar scan
as I checked in books
was soothing.
Yup, I was a
serious nerd,
but sometimes
steady work and
silence are just what
you need to clear
your head and reset.

A large stack of books
plunked onto the counter.

"I have to admit,
this is less sexy
than I thought
being a librarian
would be like,"
Artie teased.

"The media
exaggerates the
glam for sure."

"How are you,
Iza? And don't
shrug again
because Apollo
is worried (otherwise
he wouldn't have asked
me if I knew how you
are)."

I sighed, picking
at the wood grain
with my fingertip,
trying to decide
how much to say.

Artie looked over
each shoulder before
leaning closer,
"No one is in here;
tell me everything.
You can't keep
all of this inside."

I nodded and then
started at the beginning,
before Everleigh,
and then caught her up

on the beginning of Everleigh
and then finally emptied
out my feelings on Lana
about her methods
to her crazy refusal to
let me go.

"Wait," Artie said,
causing me to pause
in my ramble,
"you got accepted
into the final round
of the writing contest?"

"I guess? But I haven't
been contacted."

"Did you check your
spam folder?"

"Why would I? I got the
first email," I said.

"*Always* check your spam
folder. It's a black hole
for important non-spam

correspondence."
Artie motioned towards
the computer.
"Check it!"

"You don't think that
line was just more of
Lana's mind games?"

Artie deadpanned,
hitting me with
an unrivaled RBF
I logged in to my email.

Sure enough there was a (1)
in the spam folder.

> **You've made it into
> the final round. Please
> send your full manuscript
> no later than the twenty-ninth
> of November.**

"Well?" Artie asked.
"You were right," I grinned,
"always check the spam folder."

"After your work-study,
go make a battle plan
with your advisor. But, Iza,"
Artie said, "Lana's methods
suck but she has a point.
You are extremely gifted
and you have options.
Why not pursue *both*?"

"Really?" I questioned.

Artie nodded enthusiastically,
"You're too talented to settle."

I'd boxed myself;
I was Iza the violinist
and I'd always believed
that was enough. I hadn't
even thought to want more
and the realization that
I wanted more,
more was an option,
made my wings twitch
aching to be stretched
out and allowed to
flap into flight.

59

Artie's pep talk
combined with
Apollo's unfaltering support
had me pumped.

And my talk with
my advisor was the
icing on the cake.
She was pleased
with my progress
and displeased
with Lana's antics.

I was advised that
Lana would be
dealt with but in
the meantime to
continue playing
and writing.

"You have options
with these two
talents," my advisor
theorized, "and yes,

when you're at a
university,
you would focus
on one and minor
in the other,
but at Everleigh
the broader the abilities
the more desirable
you'll be. Can I be
candid with you, Iza?"

I nodded but
my gut clenched.
It was just another
version of
no offense but [insert insult].

"Good, could you close the door?"

I complied wordlessly.

"I know your parents
didn't sign off on you
joining Everleigh but
I admire determination.
You've got guts, Iza,

and I want you to win;
and you will
if you don't give up."

I tensed, unsure
of where this was going
or what I should say
but my advisor raised
a hand as if to stop
the obvious panicked
monologue in its tracks.

"I haven't uttered
a word of this. I just
want you to know
that I know. Many
people have similar
circumstances and they
just give up. No one
should stop you from
achieving your dreams.
Just stay out of trouble
until you're no longer
a minor, which is
early December, right?"

"Yes, on the fourth," I said.

"Even if your parents,
want to pull you out,
it won't be their choice.
Do you understand?
All I need from you
is to not give up and
I'll handle the rest."

I thanked her,
swooping my heavy
backpack over my
shoulder but
feeling grounded
rather than anchored
by the weight, the
weight that represented
everything I'd done
and everything I'd have
to do to *win*.

 I would do it all.

60

A few days later I
called Granny and she
answered on the first ring,
which made me wonder
if she'd been waiting on me.

"I won't ask how you are
because I've spoken to
your idiot parents," she
said. "Iza, there comes a
time when you have to
make your own way.
God knows, I'm sorry,
I wasn't more present.
When you fight too long
you forget there's more
than the fight but I
won't let you live
thinking those two
are the only people
you have. You'll
always have me, Iza,
but look around and
I bet you'll find family."

"Yes, ma'am, I've found one."
"Hold on to them, Iza,
trust them, let them in,
and love them back.
There's no reason to
fight the fight
on your own."

"Granny," I said, sighing,
"I don't want to come
home for Thanksgiving."

"Do you have somewhere
else to go?"

"I do."

"Then go but send
me the phone number
and address; I need to
be able to find
their asses to kick
if they hurt you."

61

Up to my elbow in suds,
Apollo and I smirked
at each other.

"You look sexy in
that apron," I teased.
"You're just jealous."
"I am, it's true!"

We'd just finished
clearing off the table,
a sweet potato pie
cooling on the stove
just begging to be
cut and served.

I was happy, the
so-happy-I-could-cry
kind of *happy*.

It'd been a small
gathering;
Belinda and Artie,
(Arnold was enroute)

Apollo and I, plus
Belinda's good friend Jewel,
and Auntie Yong from next door.
It felt just like a
cheesy Hallmark movie
safe and warm and
a moment you'd miss
when it was gone
but know it'll happen again.

The doorbell rang
and I assumed it
was Arnold until
I heard the familiar
whoop whoop
belly laugh of my
granny.

"How did you..."
I couldn't even
get the words out.
Apollo wiped a
stray tear and
took my hand in his.
All I could do was
look at him, so many

things to say that
felt too soon to say.

"Don't look at me
like that," Apollo
said softly, "you'll
make me cry and
then I'll look bad
in front of Granny."

I coughed out a
giggle and hugged
him.

"Thank you," I whispered.
"Anything for you, Iza."
"Really?"
Apollo pulled back the most
solemn loving expression
across his face.
"Iza, you have to realize
that by now."
"Can I have your
piece of pie then?"
Apollo snorted.
"Absolutely not. Go hug your Granny."

Epilogue

Iza Jones went on to pass her jury.
Lana was let go and a new
prodigy violinist (with a better bedside
manner) was hired in her place.
I wasn't the only disillusioned student.

Apollo won the writing contest,
but Iza took fourth place,
just high enough to be offered
a spot in a creative writing
program affiliated with Everleigh.
Iza received a full ride and minored in music.

Tiara worked things out
with her parents.

Arnold never showed up on
Thanksgiving and Artie decided
they'd be better off as friends.

Iza didn't convince Apollo
to give her his pie
but she managed to steal a bite.

A year later, Iza still hasn't heard
from either parent but is hopeful
and thankful for the chosen family
that found her and lifted her up
time and time again.

ACKNOWLEDGEMENTS

I'd like to take a moment to thank some of the people who've had an impact on me and my writing as I began this adventure that resulted in the creation of *Plucked*. A few years back, Yong Takahashi and I had a serendipitous moment that led us to simultaneously buying each other's books. That chance encounter of the social-media kind was truly the start of me taking myself seriously as a poet. Yong then introduced me to Fictional Cafe, which really led to my becoming their 2022-2023 Poet-in-Residence, an opportunity that changed everything. I threw myself into poetry, evolving from dipping my toe in to a full-on cannonball. That growth led to being brave enough to try something new. So, thank you, Yong, for finding me, pulling the poetess out of me, and being such a wonderful, loyal, constant presence in my life. Special thanks to Jack B. Rochester for all your work on *Plucked,* from editing to brainstorming to just putting up with the moody emotional way I can sometimes be as a writer. Jean Davis, thank you for always reading my unreadable chapters and encouraging me to keep writing anyway. The opportunity to share my work with your fearless local writing group has not only really helped keep me on track, but inspired me to try weird new things with my work—like a YA coming-of-age novel in verse. I'd also like to thank my husband Nick for always believing I can do things and then not letting me not do those things when I get scared. I push past my limits and I know that is only possible due to his love and support. There have been countless other friends, family and coworkers who have also always been at my side, cheering me on, and although I cannot list you all, I hope you know that I know and appreciate all the love and positivity you bring to my life.

About the Author

After a messy divorce from music, West fell into a torrid love affair with writing. They've been somewhat happily married since 2013, when her first novel was published in partnership with Schuler's Books & Music Chapbook Press. Since then, West has indie-published multiple novels and collections of poems tackling the themes of love, redemption, cultural identity, social issues and the afterlife. West graduated from Grand Valley State University with a Bachelor's of Art in Writing in 2011 with an emphasis on fiction and poetry. She resides in Michigan with her family and can often be found reheating the tea she forgot she made or reading a good book. Or both.